The MERCENARY

THE SAVAGE SEVEN

KATHERINE GARBERA

BRAVA

KENSINGTON PUBLISHING CORP.

www.kensingtonbooks.com

BRAVA BOOKS are published by

Kensington Publishing Corp.
119 West 40th Street
New York, NY 10018

All Kensington titles, imprints and distributed lines are available at special quantity discounts for bulk purchases for sales promotion, premiums, fund-raising, educational or institutional use.

Special book excerpts or customized printings can also be created to fit specific needs. For details, write or phone the office of the Kensington Special Sales Manager: Kensington Publishing Corp., 119 West 40th Street, New York, NY 10018. Attn. Special Sales Department. Phone: 1-800-221-2647.

Brava and the B logo are Reg. U.S. Pat. & TM Off.

ISBN-13: 978-0-7582-3210-6
ISBN-10: 0-7582-3210-1

First Kensington Trade Paperback Printing: August 2009
10   9   8   7   6   5   4   3   2   1

Printed in the United States of America

Chapter One

The phone rang as Olivia Pontuf was in the middle of stripping down for a shower. It had already been a long day and it was only 10:30 A.M.

"It's Olivia," she said, answering her cell phone. Her Black-Berry was her lifeline to her old life. She relied on it. Last week she'd thought she'd lost it and had brought the entire household to a standstill until it was found. Ray had been amused, but Olivia hadn't been. Everything she had was in that phone.

"Darling, I need you to bring me a file from my office," Ray Lambert said.

She reached into the shower and turned off the water. "Okay, give me a second to go downstairs and you can tell me which one you need."

"I don't have a minute to waste while you do whatever it is you do to fill your day," Ray said.

"I was getting in the shower, Ray, I trust you don't want me to walk naked through our home," Olivia said. Their home was a large estate house in an affluent suburb of Johannesburg. She really had no problem with nudity, but the three security guards who lived with them creeped her out a bit.

"Okay, but hurry."

She bit her lip to keep from reminding him that she had just said she'd hurry. She pulled on her thick terry bathrobe and walked out of her bedroom suite and downstairs to Ray's home office.

He said nothing while she made her way downstairs and she told herself that one of the things she'd always liked about Ray was that he didn't waste time with small talk.

The room was darkly appointed and smelled faintly of the Cuban cigars that Ray liked to smoke after dinner. "I'm here."

"About time," he muttered. "Go to my desk and open the middle drawer."

"Middle, middle? Or left middle?" she asked.

"Middle," he said. Ray seemed tense, which wasn't like him. He was usually relaxed and charming when he dealt with her. She'd seen him get short tempered with help or with service people who didn't meet his standards, but never with her.

"It's locked," she said.

"Dammit. There is a key on the credenza behind you in the bottom of the Zen rock garden," he said.

She turned around and saw the garden; she used the little rake to move the sand around until she exposed the key. She pulled it out and wiped it off on her robe before fitting into the lock.

"Okay, I've got the drawer opened."

"The folder I need is in a black envelope. Do you see it?"

She rooted around in the drawer, uncovering the envelope in the back. It was padded and thick. She resisted the urge to linger in the drawer and see what else was important enough for Ray to lock away.

"I have it."

"Great. Have Burati drive you to the mines. I need that file as quickly as you can get here."

"I guess a shower is out," she said.

"Yes, Olivia, some things are more important than appearance."

Feeling like she'd been slapped, she was silent. "I'm well aware of that, Ray."

"I'm sorry, darling. I just need that file. Please bring it as quickly as you can."

"Of course, I'll be there as soon as possible," she said.

"Excellent. Bye."

He hung up and Olivia knew she had to face the truth about this new life of hers.

She knew she had a life many would envy. She had grown up among the crème de la crème of European society, and moving from London to Johannesburg (or Jo'burg, as the locals called it) had seemed very exciting.

The reality of life here in Jo'burg was so different from what she'd imagined. The beauty of South Africa was marred for her by the constant threat of violence and crime. She couldn't jog in the early hours as she'd always done at home but instead had to wait until mid-morning when it was safer.

She wasn't a health nut but had found her habits made her life here seem more normal. And she relied on them to keep her sane.

Sure, she had a lot of social events to keep her busy and, as always, she was working on one of her fiction books about Krissie Carmichel, girl-spy. But there were also lots of bodyguards and trained attack dogs that were always nearby to keep her safe. Ten-foot-high fences surrounded the lush, leafy green residential neighborhood they lived in.

And she'd said yes to Ray's offer of marriage because he was wealthy, good looking, and moved in the same circles she did. Now she was having second thoughts.

Ray worked almost every day from before sunrise, leaving their home with his bodyguards Nels and Mumba and not returning until well after the cocktail hour. She was doing her best to fit in here, but the shopping malls closed at three, which limited her outings, and her charity work was also limited to only daylight hours.

Her work seemed stymied lately. She attributed it to the move. Moving always threw her off her writing groove.

While the people she'd met were nice, the constant threat of crime and having to always stay vigilant was wearing her down. That was why today she'd had enough.

She took a brief shower and dressed quickly in a Chanel pantsuit. Despite the fact that she knew time was of the essence, she took ten minutes to put on some makeup; she felt naked if she went out of the house without eyeliner and lipstick on.

"Going somewhere, ma'am?" Burati asked.

"Just running this folder up to Mr. Lambert at the mines," she said.

"I will have the car brought around," Burati said. His accent was lyrical and she liked to listen to him talk.

"I'd like to try driving on my own this time, Burati," she said. She needed to be alone for a little while. Her car was equipped with bulletproof glass and very safe.

"I will call Mr. Lambert and verify that."

"No, Burati, you will not. I am perfectly capable of getting myself safely to Cullinan and back." She disliked that the bodyguard treated her like a dummy. She felt his constant disdain every time she asked him to do something. If it wasn't for her writing, this world would be strangling her right now. She was a grown woman and had already figured out that she needed to make this situation work.

Burati nodded and left. She found her keys and hurried out of the house, guessing that the bodyguard would go behind her back, call Ray anyway, and probably end up trailing her all the way to Cullinan.

Leon Burati didn't exactly enjoy his job protecting Ms. Pontuf, but Phillip Michaels had been clear that protecting her came before collecting evidence on Ray Lambert. So the Soweto native had done it. Burati had taken the job for Lambert almost three years ago. His kid brother Thomas was working on the inside of Lambert's illegal operation. Both of the brothers were working to shut down the man—Ray Lambert—who had been responsible for the deaths of their father and older brothers.

No one knew that Thomas and Burati were related. They'd been very careful to keep that connection hidden, and for the most part that had worked in their favor. And Phillip—one of the executives from the diamond consortium—wanted to catch Lambert and his cohorts in the act. Phillip was gathering information from both sides of Lambert's operations and from his home life.

The diamond consortium was very aware that the output at Onyx Diamond Group was kept at the bare minimum and yet there were mining shafts that were constantly being closed or abandoned, which shouldn't have happened that frequently.

Now that he knew where Lambert hid the key to his locked drawer, Burati could go through the desk while Ms. Pontuf was gone. Being a bodyguard to the fiancée of a man whose illegal actions had put the Soweto people in danger wasn't exactly rewarding, but Burati was a patient man and would do whatever he had to until there was enough evidence to put Lambert away for life.

He let himself into the den and found the key where Olivia had left it in the Zen rock garden. The little garden had a place of honor on the corner of Lambert's credenza.

Burati opened the desk drawer and took photos of everything in there with his BlackBerry. He'd send them all to Phillip as soon as he was done.

His mobile rang before he could send the photos.

"It's Thomas. I'm at the mine and I've got the photos and the rocks that he's been selling. But something is going down. Mr. Ray seems very tense."

"Careful, brother. You shouldn't call from the mine. His people are very loyal."

"You worry too much. I can handle Mr. Ray. I'm leaving now. I will meet you in Pretoria."

"I will be there in two hours. Take your time and don't do anything to raise his suspicions."

"I won't," Thomas said. "Be cool, brother. Everything we've worked for is about to bear fruit."

Thomas disconnected the call. Burati offered a quick prayer to Allah that his brother wouldn't do anything stupid and would make it to Pretoria alive. Burati had arranged for Thomas to work on the inside of Lambert's illegal operation because he needed more information about how the actual illegal mining was done.

The many deaths at the Onyx mine were another red flag that had brought the mining operation to the diamond consortium's attention. The other mines in Africa didn't have the mortality rate that Onyx did.

Burati finished up in Lambert's den and put everything back as it had been. Then he locked the drawer and hid the key.

He walked into the hallway and sent the photos to Phillip's e-mail account. Phillip acknowledged the e-mail and mentioned he would contact Burati soon. Burati hoped now they would have enough evidence to arrest Lambert. Phillip had promised Burati a job at the Onyx Mining Group's main offices running labor relations.

Labor relations was something that Burati was very interested in. He was always looking for ways to improve his fellow villagers' quality of life. And he knew in a position of power he could make a real difference in the Soweto ghetto.

Burati had grown up in the worst ghetto near Jo'burg, Soweto. Though parts of the area had been revitalized, the section where his family lived was still a maze of cardboard boxes and dying HIV babies. He had gotten himself and his brother out as soon as he could. But Burati vowed he would save his entire village.

Chapter Two

Olivia had called her mother last night, when her parents were in port on their cruise. Olivia needed some advice about marriage and her fears, but her mother simply said that Ray was a good catch. Audrey Pontuf thought her daughter needed time to adjust to living in South Africa. "Give your new life a chance before you run back home," her mom had said.

Olivia was determined to do just that.

One of Olivia's school friends, Anna Sterling, had just gotten married. Anna was someone who always adjusted well to any situation. Without thinking twice about it, Olivia picked up her mobile phone and dialed Anna's number.

"Sterling here."

"Anna, hello. It's Olivia."

"Hi, Ola. What's up? Do you have another spy-girl question for me?" Anna asked.

"Um, not exactly. You helped me immensely with that plot glitch I had for Krissie. Do you have a few minutes to talk about something personal?" The problem with her plot had been fixed, but she was still stuck in chapter four.

Olivia could hear the sounds of loud music blaring in the background. Anna must be working on her computer.

"Sure thing," Anna said. "What's on your mind?"

"Marriage."

"I'm hardly an expert."

"Well, you're the only one I can talk to about this. I tried speaking to my mother, but that was a lost cause."

"I am only just married. Jack and I aren't exactly a conventional couple."

Anna was married to a mercenary—a gun for hire. While Olivia knew she'd never be comfortable with that kind of man, he was perfect for her friend. Olivia needed a certain level of sophistication and refinement from her men, which Ray delivered nicely. Anna worked in the shadowy world of spies and agents and having Jack for a husband made a lot of sense.

"You know more about marriage than I do."

"Okay, what do you want to know?"

"Um . . . I'm not sure if it's simply living here in Jo'burg or if Ray has changed."

"Do you like South Africa?" Anna asked.

Sometimes she liked it. Despite the poverty and unrest left by the end of apartheid, Olivia was safe enough in her insular world. She knew that. It was simply that she was tired of always having someone by her side. She knew that she had to have guards, because many of her acquaintances here did, but enough was enough.

"It is one of the most fascinating places I've ever lived, but it's hard to balance the constant threat of violence with the beauty. I'm not sure if I like it."

"You might think about joining one of those meet-up groups. There are plenty of expats there."

"I have thought about it, but Ray likes me to stay close to home or take a bodyguard with me."

Anna said nothing.

"I sound like I've lost my backbone, don't I?"

"Yes, you do."

Olivia had relied on Ray for much of her support during the last month. Their engagement wasn't really a love match, but they were fond of each other. Her mother had always said that was enough to make a good marriage last.

"I guess I've answered my own question."

"What was the question? You sound lost, Ola, and that's not like you."

"I'm thirty, Anna. You know what that means?"

"That you aren't young and impulsive anymore," Anna said.

"Exactly. I'm ready for my life to begin."

"Don't discount the years you've already had. Your life has been pretty exciting."

"I'm not, but I want a husband who cherishes me and a family of my own," Olivia said. The drive to the mines outside of Cullinan made her feel a bit more normal. Getting away from the guards in Sandton, the suburb where she lived, was what she needed. She liked her new life, she thought.

Really, she did.

"I never felt that way," Anna said quietly.

Anna had been kidnapped as a child, something that Olivia realized had shaped her friend into the woman she was today—a woman who didn't really trust in the future. It made sense that Anna wouldn't have been thinking about kids before her marriage.

"Even now?" Olivia asked.

"It's worse now. The work I'm doing with Jack's group . . . it makes me realize how very vulnerable we all are."

"You know, that's part of what I'm feeling here in South Africa. There is a definite feeling that I'm never really safe."

"Can you live with that? You've always had your father and brothers. You seemed very secure in your life."

Olivia laughed. "Not really secure. I guess I picked up my mother's acting skills."

Anna laughed too. "Probably."

She felt a hundred percent better having talked to her friend. "Thank you."

"I don't think I did anything, but you're welcome."

"You distracted me on my drive to the mines."

"Why are you going to the mines?"

"Ray needed a file he'd left at home," Olivia said.

"Do you do that often?"

"Not really, in fact he's never invited me out before. I've been begging for a tour," she said.

She'd thought that the diamond mine would make an excellent setting for one of her spy-girl books. But so far Ray didn't want to discuss his job and he had been pretty adamant that the diamond cartel would have to approve any idea she had. Her cousin was married to an executive with the diamond consortium, so Olivia figured she could use that inside track to get her book idea approved. Besides, things always worked out for her.

"I'm almost there . . . hang on a sec." Olivia couldn't be certain, but she thought she saw Ray's Mercedes off to the side of the road. She slowed her car as she saw his car on the other side of the road. There was a barrier in the middle of the road, so she pulled off on her own side.

"Sure—is anything wrong?"

"I'm not certain. Ray's Mercedes is on the side of the road," she said, straining to see over to the other side. "Well, I think his car is. Let me call you back."

"Okay. Be careful, Olivia."

"I will be. There's no one out here."

"But if his car is on the side of the road, then someone may have forced him to stop. Don't hang up. Stay on the phone with me."

"What can you do from D.C.?"

"I'm in London."

"Still hours away," Olivia said.

"Jack has men closer. If you need help, I will send someone."

"Thanks, Anna. I'm getting out of the car now."

Olivia checked to make sure there was no other traffic and there wasn't. Since the two-lane highway only led to the mine entrance, there wasn't a lot of traffic on it. She opened her door and walked across the single lane to the barrier in the middle.

"Is it Ray's car?" Anna asked.

"Definitely," she said. She recognized his signature key ring dangling in the ignition. "I'm going to climb over the barrier and see if I can find him."

"Be careful."

"You already said that," Olivia said. She was worried. Maybe leaving Burati at home hadn't been her smartest decision. So much for having to prove she was independent. She held her phone loosely in her left hand and carefully sat down on the barrier and then swung her legs over to get to the other side.

She approached Ray's car and noticed that the engine was still idling. That didn't seem like a good sign. Where was Ray?

"He left the car running," she said into the phone.

"That's odd. Is there anyone else around?" Anna asked.

Olivia looked out in the distance to the mountains and thought she saw the figures of two people, though at this distance she couldn't be sure.

"I don't know."

A shot rang out and one of the figures fell to the ground.

"Was that a gunshot?" Anna asked.

"Yes. Someone was shot. What should I do?" Olivia asked.

"Get out of there. Get back in your car," Anna said.

Olivia ran back across the street and climbed the barrier with little care for her pantsuit this time. She got behind the wheel of her vehicle and locked the doors. She just sat there shaking. What if Ray had been shot? Oh my God. What was she going to do?

"Olivia?"

"Sorry, yes?"

"Are you okay?"

"No. I'm worried about Ray . . . I don't know what to do."

"You need to get out of there and call the Cullinan authorities."

"Okay, I'll call you back."

"No, don't do that. I will call the authorities. You just stay on the other line."

Olivia put the car in drive and continued up the road to the turnabout and then sat there watching from a distance. The shooter was moving.

"I think the shooter is coming back toward Ray's car. Should I get closer and try to identify him?"

"Yes," Anna said. "Jack is on the line with the authorities. Are you on the property of Onyx Diamonds?"

"Yes," Olivia said.

"She is," Anna said to Jack. "Try and get closer to the shooter. Does your cell phone have a camera in it?"

"Yes, of course. Should I take a photo of him?"

"Definitely, and then send it to me. We have an extensive network and I will be able to tell you who it is."

"Thanks, Anna."

"No problem. Be careful."

"I'm in my car. What could happen?" Olivia said.

"He has a gun. Is your car bulletproof?"

"Yes, of course. Most cars here are because of the violence. Oh my God, can you believe I live in a place like this?"

"It's okay, you are safe. Just take the photo and then get out of there."

She drove slowly toward Ray's car. She was fairly certain the shooter had seen her. It would be impossible for him not to, with the lack of traffic out here. But she was determined to get a photo of the man. This man might have killed Ray.

She saw the man get to the car and sped up. She slowed as she approached. The man raised his gun and she raised her phone, not really thinking about anything except pushing the shutter button so that she'd have a picture of the man.

Her foot slid off the gas as she realized she was looking into the eyes of a cold-blooded killer. And then her heart stopped as she recognized her fiancé as the man holding the gun.

"Oh my God!"

She heard Anna's voice coming loudly over the phone, which she had dropped, but she couldn't pick up the phone. All she could do was stare at Ray until he lifted the gun toward her and she snapped out of her fog. She found the gas and stomped on the pedal, speeding away.

Oh. My. God.

Ray Lambert, her darling fiancé and the man everyone said was a total catch, was a murderer and he was going to kill her, she thought.

She'd seen it in his eyes. She couldn't think of anything but getting as far away from him as possible, but then panic set in and she started to worry.

What was she going to do?

Where would she go?

She had given up her life in London and her parents were currently on a world cruise. Finding them and getting back her old life would be nearly impossible.

She felt shattered and lost. She was shaking so hard she

couldn't keep on driving, so she pulled off the road once she reached the busy highway that would lead her back to her home.

She sat there for a minute, breathing deeply and trying to figure out what she could do next.

Chapter Three

Kirk Mann wasn't a people person. So that made him perfectly suited to his job as part of the Savage Seven. He was actually second in command and his specialty without fail was as a sniper.

He didn't work with a scout because they didn't have enough extra manpower to have someone designated that way on their team. There were only six of them. When he'd been in the U.S. Marines he had relied heavily on his sniper scout, Joe Gibbs, but that was a lifetime ago. And Joe was dead now. Kirk sometimes thought that Joe's ghost was with him on his missions.

Today he was in another unstable republic in Africa—this time he was killing the deposed president of a corrupt "republic." This part of the world changed leadership the way models changed their clothes at a fashion show. Kirk had spent a lot of time here.

They were working for the new government run by a man in a large African country most people in the States had never heard of. The Savage Seven had no political alliance and worked for the highest bidder. Kind of like Blackwater, except smaller and choosier about who they worked for. Jack Savage, their leader, took jobs in places that paid well.

"Are you taking the shot or what?" Jack asked in Kirk's ear.

Jack was halfway around the world in London at their headquarters, watching the setup through the camera mounted to Kirk's helmet. The reminder that he wasn't alone was the one reassurance that Kirk liked.

"Give me a second."

"What are you waiting for?" Jack asked. "Wind?"

"Yes. There was a slight gust a minute ago. I want one shot."

"That's what you are known for," Jack said.

"True that," Kirk said. He pulled out an anemometer—a handheld weather station, and waited for his reading to come back. There wasn't much difference between where he was and where the target was, but Kirk had always been a careful shooter. He had his shot lined up. He glanced down at the anemometer and made the adjustments to his trajectory to account for the wind.

He was in a run-down apartment building that ran along the alleyway from the headquarters for the Al Tarvaani faction. They were a group of Muslim fundamentalist who had been trying for years to reclaim land in this part of the world, which had been theirs centuries ago.

Kirk didn't care what their beef with the current government was. He did care that he got this job done and kept moving forward. After a while he realized that when he stood still the world didn't make sense to him.

"I'm lined up now," Kirk said.

"You are good to go," Jack said.

Kirk was not the only member of the team in-country. JP "Laz" Lazarus was downstairs in a car waiting for a quick escape. Laz and Kirk had done this same job many times and worked together like a well-oiled machine.

"Laz?" Kirk asked.

"I'm ready when you are."

Kirk took a breath and held it, letting out half of it he lightly squeezed the trigger as Karzon—his target—stepped away from the table where he had been sitting. He stood and leaned over the table pointing at something on the map he had been studying with his men.

Kirk exhaled and pulled the trigger. He watched as the bullet struck his target between the eyes and the man fell back into his chair. He was dead. Kirk always struck true and lethal. He watched for a moment through his sight to confirm his target was dead.

"Tango down," Kirk said.

"Copy that," Savage said. "Now move."

Back in the Corps he would have had to get a DNA sample to affirm he'd hit the right target, but with Savage there wasn't really any paperwork trail. He packed up his Barrett .50 sniper rifle. Kirk grabbed his bag as the men with Karzon scrambled to their feet, firing bullets toward his location. But he suspected they didn't really know which apartment building he was in because none of the bullets came close to him.

Kirk was down the three flights of stairs, out onto the street, and into the waiting car in less than sixty seconds. As soon as Kirk was in the back, Laz took off, driving not like a man with escape on his mind but slowly through the light traffic. They kept moving away from their target toward the airport. Kirk didn't look up or around, but concentrated on putting his weapon away.

He was a weapon of war and had been for the better part of his adult life. He was a tool that was used for the purpose that it had been made. Hammers didn't think about the nails they put in the wood and Kirk Mann didn't stop to think about the man he'd killed. But sometimes, Kirk felt all those deaths added up.

"How'd it go?" Laz asked.

"Same as always. Sweet and clean."

"You okay?"

"Perfect, why?"

"I don't know. Just checking. This is our third operation in a row . . ."

The very last thing he wanted to do was discuss how much time he hadn't taken off with Laz while Jack was on the line.

"Yeah, so this is what we do—keep the world a safer place."

"Hell, yeah," Laz said. "But everyone else has had a few weeks off—

"And you want some, too?"

"Yes. I've got a sweet little piece waiting for me Stateside, but I can't get back to her until *you* take a day off."

"Am I cramping your style, loverboy?" Kirk asked.

"Screw you," Laz said.

"Boys," Savage said.

"Yes, sir," Kirk said.

"Laz's love life will have to stay on hold. I need you two to head to Johannesburg ASAP."

"I'm surprised. I was thinking we'd hit Somalia next," Laz said. "All those pirate attacks off their coast."

Kirk was, too. Lately there had been a lot of attacks on shipper freighters and yachts in the Indian Ocean.

"Not yet. I'm in talks with our contacts in the area," Savage said.

Kirk wasn't surprised. The pirates operating off the coast of Somalia were out of control and the governments who were being affected there were all trying to put an end to it. But jurisdiction and fuck-all stood in their way. So men like the Savage Seven would be the ones to restore peace there. *Ooo-rah.* The companies that were trying to ship oil and other freight through the region had to be good and pissed at the hijackings that had taken place over the last six months.

"Why Jo'burg?"

"Anna's on the horn with a high-profile witness to a murder. It happened on Onyx Diamond Group property, so the local authorities have no jurisdiction."

"What do you want us to do?"

"It appears the shooter was the woman's fiancé," Savage said.

"Bodyguard and extraction duty?" Laz asked. God, he hated doing that kind of thing. "We aren't babysitters. We are guns for hire."

"I know that," Jack said.

"Why can't Liberty Investigations handle this?" Kirk asked. He really didn't want to have to go to Johannesburg right now. "Send her to her embassy and tell them to keep her safe."

"Liberty doesn't have anyone close enough. Look, she's scared and freaking out and she's a friend of Anna's. Just keep her safe until we can get there," Savage said.

"What's her name?" Kirk asked.

"Olivia Pontuf. She's an American but recently lived in London. She's been in Johannesburg for the last six weeks with her fiancé, Ray Lambert, managing director of Onyx Diamond Mines."

"Do you have mission specs on this?"

"I'm sending a file to you both right now."

Kirk received the file on his satellite smartphone and opened it up. The woman was beautiful. Breathtaking, really, even on the tiny display screen of his smartphone.

"Well, hello," Laz said. "Forget about my needing time off."

Kirk laughed. Laz was always on the make. Of all the guys on the team, he was the closest thing they had to a playboy. Most of the men were like Kirk, more interested in the job.

Kirk didn't know if Olivia Pontuf was anything like Anna Sterling. If she was, then Kirk could understand Laz getting excited over her. Anna was one of the few women Kirk had met in the last few years who had held his interest.

Looking at that woman, he wondered why she'd thought about getting married. She didn't look like the wife-and-mother type. But then who was he to judge someone by their looks? He remembered his sweet little wife—Abby. He'd once wanted a family, but that desire had died with his young wife and stillborn son more than twenty years ago.

That event and the USMC had shaped him into the man he was today.

Chapter Four

Olivia couldn't stop panicking as she drove back to the house she'd shared with Ray—a murderer. She tried in her mind to justify what he'd done. Maybe he had some sort of explanation that would make it all okay.

But she highly doubted that. He'd pointed a gun at her. How was he going to explain that?

He'd killed a man. No matter how she sliced it, she couldn't forget that. Anna had promised to send a man from her husband's team to protect her.

The irony of this situation wasn't lost on Olivia. Ray, the one man she'd relied on to protect her in this hostile, beautiful world, was now the one she needed protection from.

She still had the envelope he'd asked her to bring to the mines and she had nothing else. Her handbag. A nice designer clutch that held only her lipstick, coin purse, and one credit card. Hardly enough to get her out of the country. And though Anna had said to go directly to the airport, Olivia knew she needed clothes and more money.

She drove with a purpose, no longer enjoying the scenery

but instead flying through the city streets until she reached her residential neighborhood. She pushed the button that activated the gate to her community.

The guard smiled and waved at her and she forced herself to wave back. She felt her breath getting shorter as images kept flashing through her mind. Images of Ray shooting someone—she still didn't know who. And images of Ray glaring at her as she drove past his car, aiming his gun at her.

He would have killed her.

Her hands started to shake and she almost lost it, but there was no time for that. She forced everything to the back of her mind and found a kind of calm that she knew was false. She only had to keep it together until she got to the airport. Then she would get on the plane and get the hell out of South Africa.

She pulled into the circle drive of the house she shared with him. Burati came to the front door as she came up the walk.

Her bodyguard . . . would he protect her? She had no idea, and she didn't want to take a chance that Ray may have called him and asked him to keep her here.

"Shall I bring the car around back, Ms. Pontuf?" Burati asked.

She shook her head. "I'll be going back out soon. I have a lunch date with a friend of mine."

"Very well, ma'am."

"Burati? Has Mr. Lambert called?"

"No, ma'am."

Olivia nodded. She felt safer knowing that Burati hadn't talked to Ray. He might not like her, but she didn't think he'd kill her.

She walked calmly into the house, not wanting to alert the guard if what he said was true. She went straight to her office and found her backup flash drive, then she went to her closet and took down her Louis Vuitton duffel. She grabbed clothes randomly and tossed them in. Then she changed her shoes from the heels she had on to her running shoes. She went to the bathroom and grabbed toiletries off the vanity.

And walked out the door. She was halfway down the stairs when she heard the rumble of Burati's voice. She didn't speak Afrikaans well enough to understand what he was saying. But she didn't take any chances. She went back into Ray's office and opened that middle drawer again. This time she took everything in there and put it in her duffel.

She had no idea if it was important or not, but she wanted everything she could find on Ray. Anything she could use to figure out what was going on.

She walked into the hallway, pulled her sunglasses on, and made her way to the front door. In the large foyer with its marble floors and gilt-framed artwork she heard Burati's voice.

"Ms. Pontuf?"

She kept walking. This foyer represented what she'd always thought of as security. How foolish had that been? Things couldn't protect her. Money couldn't protect her, either, she realized. She walked out the door, hearing Burati behind her but very afraid to stop and talk to the man.

She got in the car as he came to the door. She noticed he had his hand on the butt of his handgun as she climbed into the car and locked the doors. Her car was bulletproof and she knew Burati wouldn't waste a bullet on the car.

She started the engine and put the car in drive. She wondered if they'd let her leave the compound. She didn't worry about that right now. She just had to get away. If Burati had been alerted to what had happened, that meant Ray knew she'd seen something.

Her mobile phone rang and she glanced at the caller ID. *Ray.*

Should she answer it?

She had no idea what to do, but went ahead and answered

the call because she needed to know what he was going to do. If he believed she had seen him kill a man or if she'd simply driven by him and noticed the gun.

"Hello," she said, trying to sound calm and as if there was nothing out of the ordinary about her day.

"Olivia," Ray said. "Where are you? I need you to go to the house and wait there for me."

"I can't do that, Ray."

"Why not? You know that Jo'burg isn't safe for you on your own. You could turn down the wrong street and find yourself in a bad neighborhood."

"Or I could just walk into our home and find you waiting for me."

"You could, but I won't hurt you," Ray said.

"You pointed a gun at me." Olivia realized she didn't know Ray. Not the way she should have before she'd agreed to marry him.

"Darling, I didn't know it was you. That man was trying to kill me, and I was afraid you might be his accomplice," he said. "You're clearly distraught, go back home and we'll talk about it. I'm not sure it's safe for you. Everyone knows you are my fiancée."

"I can't," she said. "I'm leaving Johannesburg."

"Where are you going? Burati said you'd packed a bag," Ray said.

She took a deep breath. "I . . . a friend of mine is going through a tough time and she asked me to come and stay with her."

"Which friend?" he asked.

"A school chum . . . Anna Sterling. I don't believe you know her."

"Where is she?"

Olivia knew better than to say London. So she stuck with the truth to a certain extent. "Washington D.C. I'll call you when I get there and let you know when I can come back. Maybe you will have taken care of the threat to yourself by then."

She wondered if she should have kept that information to herself. What if he did something to Anna?

She'd have to call Anna and warn her.

"Olivia?"

"Yes, Ray."

"I still need that envelope you were bringing to me," he said. He sounded aggravated with her now.

"I left it with the guard at the gate of the Onyx mines." Olivia usually didn't hold with lying, except maybe a little white lie when a friend had made an unfortunate fashion choice.

In this case she figured that Ray didn't deserve the truth from her. And he'd killed a man. She didn't care what the circumstances were; she knew she couldn't marry a man who was a murderer.

She wondered if this was a onetime crime or if Ray had done this before. She knew that the diamond mine property was private and Ray wasn't answerable to anyone except the diamond consortium.

"Did you?" he asked.

"Yes, Ray, I did. And now I have to go. You know I don't like to talk on my mobile while I'm driving," she said, hanging up the phone.

She put the phone on the passenger seat and tried to think who she could go to with the evidence she had. The U.S. Embassy had no authority over the diamond mines. The only governing body that did was the diamond consortium. Her cousin Amy's husband Phillip was on the board of the consortium. They lived in Denmark, so they weren't exactly local.

But she thought she might have to give them a call once she was safe. She wasn't going to be able to think or really take a deep breath until she was out of Jo'burg. She just didn't feel safe here.

She felt tears burn the back of her eyes, but she didn't cry. Wouldn't allow herself to be that weak. Nothing bad had happened to her. She'd witnessed Ray doing something unspeakable, but that didn't mean she had to break down. She could keep it together. She repeated that to herself until the words became the truth and she calmed down.

Chapter Five

"Fuck!" Ray Lambert threw his mobile phone against the wall as Olivia hung up on him. It shattered into several pieces just as his carefully ordered world was doing. He didn't need this right now. Not from Olivia. She was part of his perfect world. The one that couldn't be touched by the dirtiness of his life here at the mines.

"Dammit. Anita, get in here."

"Yes, sir?" Anita, his secretary, asked as she stood in the doorway to his office.

"I need a new mobile phone."

She nodded. "I have two replacements in my supply cabinet, Mr. Lambert. If you give me your old phone, I can send it back to the dealer."

He gestured to the floor where the pieces still remained. She looked at it and then got down on her knees to pick up the pieces. "What shall I say happened to it?"

"It fell off my belt when I was in the mine," he said.

"No problem," Anita said. She left his office and returned a few minutes later with a brand-new phone. She handed it to him along with his SIM card.

He took the replacement BlackBerry and put the SIM card in the back. He hit the power button and waited. The phone worked fine and he dismissed Anita from his office.

"Go with her, Nels," he said to his bodyguard. The other man left his office.

The Onyx Diamond Group was part of a larger diamond-mining consortium and Ray had been working for them since he'd come to South Africa nearly twenty years ago. He had started a lucrative sideline of off-the-record mining five years ago. The diamonds he sold on the black market provided a nice extra income that he used for gambling, women, and the good life.

He didn't have to worry about what he spent and what he lost, thanks to the two-pronged profit stream he had created at this mine in Cullinan. He'd worked his ass off trying to figure how to keep his bosses at the consortium happy and how to take care of the huge debts he had from gambling.

Every single time he got caught up, he'd play a big game and almost win enough to be satisfied and then lose. Luckily he'd always been able to come back here and replenish his bank accounts.

The deal with Olivia angered him. He liked her and had planned to have a family with her. She was going to be the perfect cover to his other life. He hadn't really planned on getting engaged, but once he'd met her and realized she was the cousin of Phillip Michaels, the idea had come to him. Being in the family with one of the executives of the Diamond Consortium would definitely be a perk.

And now that was all screwed up. Part of it was Olivia. He had no idea how much she'd seen this afternoon. Judging by her pale face and the way she'd gunned her engine to get away from him, he had to assume she'd seen him shoot

Thomas and he had aimed his gun at her. If her car hadn't had bulletproof windows, he would have shot. But wasting a bullet hadn't seemed like the best idea.

In retrospect he may have been able to scare her enough to make her crash her car or something. He should have thought that through, but he'd panicked.

Killing a man was never an easy thing for him to do. And Thomas had been young, which made it a bit harder. Somehow, for him, if a criminal was older it was easier.

And that was the other part of the problem. His black-market operation worked because he controlled the volume of the diamonds that were sold there. He made damned sure that they were well under the radar of the consortium, but Thomas had been slipping extra diamonds out of the mine to fund some sort of rebel faction in his hometown. That stinking ghetto of Soweto.

And that had been unacceptable. Ray didn't tolerate thievery.

Now Lars Inglessin and Phillip Michaels were on Ray's back about the leakage from this mine and were both coming here to personally make sure the operation was back on track.

Phillip was Olivia's cousin by marriage, which was going to make that entire mess a bit uncomfortable. But he'd deal with it. He always did.

The fact that Thomas had been stealing gave Ray an easy scapegoat for the stones he himself had been funneling out, but he wasn't sure how much Lars knew and how long he'd have to play along with Lars until the man left.

This mess wasn't what he needed right now. And with Olivia added to the mix . . . he had no idea what to do next. Of course, with Burati in the house, he didn't have to worry too much about Olivia. He'd farm the task of taking care of his fiancée to the bodyguard. Somehow Ray wasn't sure he could kill her.

Besides, he and Nels had to go back and dispose of Thomas's body.

Ray didn't panic because that wasn't the type of man he was. Instead he sat back in his chair and listed the options in his head. Perhaps getting Olivia out of the picture would be the best option. If she were dead, then he wouldn't have to worry about her going to the authorities. To be honest, he wasn't sure what the authorities could do to him. The Onyx Diamond Group policed their own property and their own disputes.

But the diamond consortium would be angry that governments were involved in their business and they might come down hard on him.

His office phone rang and he answered it impatiently. "Lambert here."

"Mr. Ray, it's Burati. Ms. Olivia left the desk in your home office open when she left. I believe she took everything in there."

Fuck. "Thank you, Burati. Did you follow her?"

"Yes, Mr. Ray. I am in the car now. She seems to be headed toward the airport in Jo'burg."

Olivia had just helped make his mind up as to her fate. "Don't let her get on a plane. I want her out of the picture," Ray said.

"What do you mean, Mr. Ray?"

"I mean that she shouldn't talk to anyone, do you understand me? She's in danger. I had some trouble at the mine today and if she should run into the men who tried to kill me . . ."

There was silence on the line and Ray wondered if the guard understood what he wanted.

"Yes, sir, Mr. Ray."

"Good. Bring me everything she has on her."

"Yes, Mr. Ray," Burati said. "I will talk to you after I find her."

"Very well," Ray said. "No mistakes, Burati. I want this matter settled as soon as possible."

"It will be, Mr. Ray."

Ray disconnected the call. He didn't dwell on what Burati was going to do. He couldn't. He'd liked Olivia, otherwise he wouldn't have asked her to marry him. And he had enjoyed living with her. She hadn't been the sexiest woman he'd ever dated, but she had been one of the nicest.

He had a moment of silence thinking of what their life might have been. He would miss her, but she knew too much to live and he knew that she'd never keep quiet.

If he'd learned anything from the past month of living with her it was that she had a strong sense of right and wrong and the gray areas of real life didn't make sense to her.

He blamed her parents for sheltering her. As a matter of fact, it was their fault she was going to die. If they'd raised their daughter to see that there was more to the world than a cut-and-dried right and wrong, she probably wouldn't have panicked and ran.

He had a meeting in ten minutes and realized he'd sweated through his dress shirt. Dammit. He took off his shirt and realized he had dirt and dried blood on it.

Where was his head? He went into his private washroom and washed his hands and face. He sprayed on his cologne and then redressed. All the while he watched himself in the mirror.

He made damned sure that the man looking back at him was cool and calm. The Managing Director of Mining Operations wasn't a man who could be scared or not in control.

Ray had worked his way up the hard way and it took balls to operate a shadow mine under the watchful eye of the diamond consortium and not get caught. Ray had done that for the last few years with no hiccups until one of his workers had gotten greedy. But Thomas was dead now, and soon Olivia would be out of the way as well.

He walked out of the washroom confident of himself. And when he pulled his suit jacket on he realized that this morning was in the past, Olivia was in the past, and all he could do was move on.

And he would. That was what Ray Lambert did. Getting married had seemed like the next step in his plan to make himself into the successful man he'd always wanted to be, but a woman was more complicated. And Ray was revising his opinion on wives.

Mistresses were easier to control and not as needy. That was one thing he hadn't liked about Olivia. She had clung to him, expecting him to be her social network here.

And the sex hadn't been that great. In fact, since she'd moved here a few months ago, she hadn't been able to feel comfortable having sex with him.

She said she didn't feel safe with the barbed-wire fence around their neighborhood and the guards sleeping down the hall. He bet she really felt unsafe now that she was out there on her own.

It'd be so much easier for him if she broke down in one of the central Jo'burg neighborhoods. A random act of violence would be a nice neat way to tie up the problem.

Chapter Six

Olivia drove into the parking garage at the Johannesburg International Airport. She'd gotten nervous once she'd entered the city limits of Jo'burg and had called Anna. She just felt safer when she was on the phone with the other woman.

"We are sending two men to meet you in Johannesburg. Where are you?" Anna said.

"I'm at the airport."

"Good. Now get inside and go to the bar. Kirk and Laz are on their way. But their flight won't land for another hour. I want you in the public with lots of people around you," Anna said.

"I still don't know why I just didn't drive to the embassy."

"Would you feel safe there? I don't have any contacts at the embassy and neither does Jack. But if you would feel safer, then go there."

Olivia had no idea where she'd feel safer. She started to cry, just thinking about everything. "I have no idea. I'm scared, Anna."

"I know. I am scared for you. I wish I was there with you."

"Me, too," Olivia said. She took a deep breath and wiped her eyes. "Okay, I'm going into the airport."

"Good. I'll stay on the phone with you until the guys get there."

"For an hour? That's asking a lot of our friendship."

"No, it's not," Anna said.

Olivia grabbed her Louis Vuitton duffel bag and her purse and got out of her car. The parking garage was well lit but almost deserted at this time of the day. She locked her car and then walked quickly toward the airport concourse. She had no ticket. Where was she going to go? She had said D.C., but she really wanted . . . she wanted to find a safe place where she could just hide out for a long while.

"I don't have a ticket," Olivia said.

"That's fine. Just get inside. Find the armed airport guards and stay near them. If you see someone suspicious, go to the armed guards. I'm accessing the Johannesburg International Airport security cameras, so I'll be watching you, too."

"You can do that?" Olivia asked.

"Of course. I'm a whiz with computers."

Anna had always been a bit of a computer geek when they'd been at school. In fact she'd changed Olivia's grade in algebra by hacking into the school's computer network. "I forgot."

"You've got a lot on your mind today. I see you now," Anna said.

"Oh no. I changed my shoes and they don't go with this outfit."

Anna started laughing and Olivia realized how silly she must have sounded. "Well, normally, I would never wear running shoes with a suit like this."

"I know. You still look stunning."

"Sure I do. Where should I go? I think that café on the corner looks nice."

"Yes. That's good. Just sit someplace where you can minimize your exposure."

"How?"

"Get a table with your back to the wall," Anna said.

Olivia walked over to the restaurant and asked for a table in the back near the corner. She had to put the phone down to do so. In Jo'Burg no one would offer service while she was on her cell phone.

She was seated and given a menu. She lifted the handset back to her ear. "I'm sitting down."

"You're out of my camera range. Tell me what the place is like," Anna said.

"Should I move?"

"No, you're fine there. Just tell me what's in the restaurant."

"It's a regular-looking café. Most of the tables are full. My table is in the corner, so I've got walls on two sides of me."

"Good. Now, where is the kitchen?"

Olivia glanced around the diner. She placed her duffel bag by her feet and put her handbag on the table. The restaurant was typical of airport–type establishments and she saw the usual patrons at the tables: families, couples, and students. Everyone looked so normal and she felt so *not* normal.

"Olivia? Are you still there? Are you okay?"

"Sorry. The kitchen is to my left." She felt silly and foolish. To think she'd called Anna to get marriage advice a few hours earlier and now she was on the run from a man who was trying to kill her. Her own fiancé.

"Is it close?"

"Less than a hundred yards. Why?" she asked, but all she could think about was Ray waving that gun at her.

"You might need to go that way if someone comes for you," Anna said.

"Like who? I think Burati was following me, but I haven't seen him since I left my neighborhood." She wasn't cut out for this type of situation. She didn't want to have to look for an escape route. She just wanted to get on a plane and get out of here. "Should I leave Jo'burg?"

"Not today. Let our men get to you and then we will figure out what to do," Anna said. "Who is Burati?"

"My bodyguard. Ray hired him for me."

"What is his full name?" Anna asked.

"I have no idea. I never asked. That makes me seem like a rude person, doesn't it?"

"Not at all. Just relax while I do some research on men with his name. Jack is monitoring the police communication and no one has reported the shooting you saw."

"Do you think I imagined it?" she asked Anna. What if she had? She was going to feel like an idiot if that happened.

"No, I don't. I heard the shot, remember?"

"That's right," Olivia said, sighing. "This is the worst day of my life."

"Don't say that. Better to find this all out before you get married," Anna said.

"That's true. I thought Ray was my dream man."

"Why?"

"Because he had a good job, he's good looking, and he paid attention to me. You know?"

"I can understand that. But your life is changing now. And, to be fair, Ray probably is all of those things. He was just keeping part of himself from you."

"Yes, I know that. It makes me feel stupid that I didn't realize he would hide anything from me," she said.

"What do you think he hid?" Anna asked.

"Well, murder, for one."

"For one? What else?"

"I don't know, but he had a locked drawer in his desk and I took everything in it."

"Kirk and Laz will be coming to you soon. They'll watch over you and help you get the information to us so we can figure out which authorities to notify to make sure Ray can't hurt you anymore."

Olivia wanted to believe her friend, but a big part of her felt like she'd never be safe again.

Burati hung up the phone with Lambert and immediately dialed Phillip Michaels. He had to wait until the other man was out of a meeting to speak to him.

"Ms. Pontuf witnessed a killing at the mines today and Lambert wants her killed," he said as soon as Phillip had answered.

"One thing at a time. Where is Ms. Pontuf?" Phillip asked.

"She's heading to the airport. I'm in my own car following her."

"Good. I want you to pick her up at the airport and bring her to my safe house. It's in Cape Town, and I don't think Lambert will think to go there to find her."

"Yes, sir. I'll need the address."

"I will send a text message with it," Phillip said. "Now, who was killed?"

"I don't know. I spoke to Thomas this morning and he had the rocks we wanted as well as some other information. He didn't come to our arranged meeting . . ." Burati let his words trail off.

He didn't want to think about his kid brother being dead. If Thomas was dead, then Burati wouldn't rest until Lambert paid with his own life.

"I will find out as soon as I can. I will speak to Lambert as soon as we are off the phone. Did he ask you to kill Olivia?"

"Not in so many words."

"Damn, he's good about making sure he never incriminates himself."

"Yes, he is. About Thomas . . ."

"If your brother was killed, you will be compensated for his loss."

Burati made a noise.

"I know that money can't make up for the loss of a family member," Phillip said. "It's just that I have no other way to show you what your loss means to the consortium."

"Thank you, Phillip."

"You're welcome. Olivia is my wife's cousin and protecting her for me is something I appreciate you doing." Phillip was a good man, a man who Burati respected. Burati would do his best to make sure Ms. Olivia remained safe.

"I will continue to do my job. If he did kill Thomas, that simply makes me more determined to make sure he is captured and stopped," Burati said.

"We'll get him, Burati. I promise you that."

"I am at the airport and I'll call you after I have Olivia."

"Thank you."

Burati hung up the phone and sat there in the parking lot grieving for his brother. He was almost positive that Thomas had been killed today. He called his cousin Barack because he wanted backup when he went in to get Olivia. If word got back to Mr. Ray that he had taken Ms. Olivia to a safe house, Burati knew he'd be in big trouble. He needed someone who could provide backup in case things went wrong.

Barack waited for him in the departure lounge. "I'm not sure where she is, so we'll have to search all the departure gates. I'm going to see if she's purchased a ticket first."

Barack nodded and was happy to follow orders. Burati didn't think about anything except finding Olivia. He didn't dwell on the fact that his brother was dead and he was now going to be a rich man.

Kirk didn't like airports. He didn't mind flying, but airport terminals were something altogether different. Public airports were the worst. Everyone was in a hurry and not bothering to get the hell out of the way like they should. Because they were flying with weapons, he and Laz had to go through a special line at security when they arrived in Johannesburg. Laz, being the more heavily loaded down of the two of them, was going to bear the brunt of any questions.

"Stop looking like you want to shoot someone," Laz said.

Kirk snorted. He didn't want to shoot anyone. He just wanted to be out of the airport and the crowd. This many people made him cranky. And something that Savage had said on the phone a few minutes ago was making the back of his neck itch.

Regardless of whether they had wanted to do this extraction, it was their mission, and the Savage Seven never failed. And until they got to the girl, the situation wasn't in his control. He didn't like that.

"The line isn't going to move any faster no matter how much you glare."

"It might. I want the girl with us so we can relax."

Laz snorted. "You don't know the meaning of relaxation."

"That might be true, but I do know the meaning of a locked door in a secure room. That's what I want."

"Should be a piece of cake," Laz said.

Kirk nodded. Laz was fine, but Kirk needed to process the job he'd just done and find his center. Jack would laugh his ass off if he knew that Kirk did that after each kill, but it was the only way he could move on and stay sane. He had a ritual and this was messing with it. He was edgy and ready for a fight.

Not the best way to be when he had to protect a friend of Anna's.

They edged forward in the line. "What the fuck is taking so long?"

"Who knows?"

Kirk took a deep breath. "I'll get the girl while you get the car. We'll meet you out front."

"Fine. We can't test our earpieces until we clear customs," Laz said.

"What do you think of everything she saw?" Laz asked. "I know that the fiancé threatened her with a gun, but . . ."

Kirk shrugged. "That doesn't have anything to do with our job here."

"Yeah, I know. But that had to throw her. My sister's husband turned out to be a pedophile. Maureen freaked out."

Kirk shook his head. "I'm sorry, Laz. That had to be rough. Does she have to see the bastard?"

"Not anymore. I took care of that problem for her."

Kirk didn't ask any other questions. He knew what Laz meant and that was enough for him. He would've done the same if he'd had a sister. Despite the fact that he was a loner, he did take care of his own.

Of course the only family he had were the men of the Savage Seven. The line inched forward a few more feet. And Kirk couldn't take another second. The walls were closing in around him. He needed fresh air.

"You okay?" Laz asked.

He nodded. "Yeah, great."

They were waved up to the customs agent. Kirk pushed past Laz to go first, knowing his friend wouldn't care. He handed the form he had and the weapons permit to the man.

"What's the purpose of your visit?" the agent asked.

"Work."

"When will you be leaving?"

"In twenty-four hours," Kirk said.

"You have to claim your weapons with our agent."

Kirk nodded. "Welcome to South Africa, Mr. Mann. Enjoy your stay."

"Thank you."

Kirk took his passport and walked to the area where he knew he'd be able to reclaim his weapon. He wondered if that wasn't part of his problem. He felt damned naked without his gun.

Laz was right behind him. They collected their weapons and radio communication earpieces, which they both donned immediately.

"Check, check," Kirk said.

"Gotcha," Laz said.

"Savage? You on here?"

"Sure am. Where are you two?" Savage asked.

"Just outside bag claim," Kirk said. "Where is the girl?" Now that they were here, he was ready to get this mission rolling.

"She's in a café waiting for you," Jack said. "Laz, there is a car waiting under your name. I think we need to check out Olivia's car. See if it's where she left it and put a tracking device on it in case the fiancé comes to get the car."

"I'll do that," Laz said.

"I'm on my way to find the girl. I have her photo. Does she know to expect me?" Kirk asked, reviewing Olivia's photo on his BlackBerry.

"Affirmative," Jack said. "Anna's been on the phone with her since she arrived at the airport."

"Good. I'll let you know when I'm in position," Kirk said.

Laz left to find the car and do his tasks. Jack was on the line but not talking and Kirk didn't let any of that bother him. One of the things he really liked about his team was that they all pulled their own weight and could be counted on to do their jobs.

He entered the airport departure area where the restaurants were and walked toward the café where Olivia was waiting. He saw a group of students standing in the entrance area as two men who looked like professionals in his line of work pushed past the students.

"Dammit. Someone else may be interested in our girl," Kirk said.

"What? Anna, get me the footage from the airport on my screen."

Kirk didn't wait around for Savage to tell him to get in there. It stood to reason that her fiancé may have already sent a team to take her out if she saw too much.

"Hold up, Kirk," Jack said.

Kirk kept moving. He heard Jack talking to Anna. The other man's voice was completely calm. And then he heard a scream and the sound of a table being overturned as he walked into the diner.

"Shit," Jack said.

"I'm on it," Kirk said, taking off after the men who were dragging Olivia Pontuf out of the restaurant.

Chapter Seven

Olivia screamed. She yelled as loud as she could, hoping for help. She clawed at Burati's arms, trying to reach his face. He held on to her with surprising strength. She was almost numb with fear. The only thing that kept her going was the fact that she didn't want to die.

"Let me go!"

"Shut up," Burati said.

The kitchen staff all looked the other way as he dragged her through the back of the restaurant. The kitchen wasn't that busy at this time of the day and no one looked at her.

Burati said something in Afrikaans and the other men laughed. Olivia knew that no one would be coming to her aid.

"Hurry up, Leon. We need to get out of here before the authorities come."

Burati grabbed her hands and held them together. "Use that duct tape to fasten her hands, Barack."

Barack did as he was told. Olivia struggled and kicked but Burati held on to her tightly. "Stand still."

"No. I'm not going to make it easy for you to kidnap me."

Barack had her bag and her phone and she could only hope that Anna had figured out what was going on, that maybe her friend would send help . . . but a part of Olivia knew she could only rely on herself.

Olivia kicked out, trying to get Burati or Barack, but both men stepped out of her reach. She spun on her heel and ran as fast as she could. She sprinted all out through the kitchen and through the back door, which led to a hallway.

She hesitated, not sure which way to go. That hesitation cost her.

Burati's heavy hand fell on her shoulder and she was lifted over his shoulder facedown. She kicked and screamed until he slapped her hard on the ass.

"Settle down, Ms. Olivia. We don't want any extra attention."

"Screw you, Burati. This is kidnapping and illegal. Do you honestly think you will get away with this?"

"I'm not kidnapping you," he said. Walking down the hallway, she heard the door behind them open and she twisted to see who was following them.

A man with a gun and dark stubble, that was who. Olivia felt like the situation was getting worse by the second. What was she going to do? She wasn't giving up, but she didn't think she could fight this man and win.

"Freeze!" he yelled, but Burati didn't stop. "Drop the woman."

"Stay out of this," Burati responded.

Olivia tried to kick her legs and this time Burati brought his hand to her thigh, squeezing tightly until she thought she'd pass out from the pain. She didn't let that stop her, using her bound fists and punching him in the side.

"Help me!" she yelled to the man who'd entered the hallway. He was tall, dark, and scary but he seemed the lesser of two evils right now.

In the back of her mind was the thought that maybe this was the man that Anna was sending to her. "Kirk?"

He nodded, but didn't respond, and that made her feel better. And she stopped worrying about him and his position and just tried to get free.

She heard a gunshot and felt Burati flinch and fall to one side. He was off balance and she rolled off him. With her hands bound it was hard to get to her feet, but she struggled upright.

She glanced around, her long hair swinging into her face. She ached everywhere. Burati drew his gun and aimed it at Kirk, but he didn't slow down. Kirk just shot Burati in his gun hand. Burati's handgun clattered to the floor. Barack fired at Kirk, but Kirk hit the man on the side of the neck as he came up to him. The other man crumpled to the floor.

Kirk grabbed her bag and kept on moving. Burati reached for his gun, and Olivia kicked it out of his grasp. Kirk bent down next to the other man and said something that was too low for her to hear. Then he clocked Burati on the head. Both of the men were unconscious.

"Let's move," he said.

"I need my bag," she said. Searching for anything that would delay the moment when she actually left with this man. He scared her almost as much as the look in Burati's eyes had.

"I've got your bag," he said. "Laz?"

She had no idea who he was talking to. "What?"

"Be quiet and follow orders. The airport security guards are on their way. We need to get out of here quickly."

"Did Anna send you?" she asked him.

"Yes. I'm Kirk Mann. My colleague is waiting for us with a car."

"You can talk to him?" she asked, walking beside him. Actually *trotting* beside him, since he was taller than she was and walking at a fast clip. Maybe it was a good thing she'd put on her running shoes. Oh. My. God. She had almost been kidnapped. She'd seen Ray kill someone, he'd held a gun on her, and . . .

"Lady, keep up."

"Olivia," she said. "Call me Olivia."

He nodded and then said something else to someone she couldn't see. "How are you communicating with these other men?"

"We have wireless communication devices," he said glancing back at her. "I have her. Let Anna know that I will put her on the phone as soon as we are secure."

"Who are you talking to?" Olivia asked.

"My boss—Jack Savage. Listen, lady, if you could just be quiet and keep up, this will go more smoothly."

She made a face at him but clammed up. She was tired and ached from trying to escape Burati. And she realized a numbness had taken over her. She still had the duct tape around her wrists, but she figured right now that wasn't important. Getting to safety was. And there was something about Kirk Mann that made her feel safe.

Maybe it was the way he'd taken out those two men. She didn't know. She only knew that for right now she was glad he was at her side. He would keep her safe, she knew that. She trusted that.

The fact that Burati had come after her like that made it clear to Olivia that Ray realized she had seen something today. She had no idea if he knew she'd witnessed him killing a man, but she did know that he seemed to want her dead.

"We are going to need to move quickly when I open this door. Laz is waiting in the arrival car park. He will have a dark green Mercedes," Kirk said.

She nodded.

"Take my hand."

"I can't," she said, lifting her bound wrists.

He took a knife from his pocket and cut her free. He pocketed the knife and took her hand in his. His bigger one engulfed hers. But as he slid their fingers together she couldn't help but notice how strong his grip was. He wasn't going to let her go. It was an oddly comforting thought as they emerged into the regular airport traffic.

She had that feeling of her life becoming some kind of surreal foreign movie. When she'd watched those films it had always seemed a bit daring and exciting to think of her ordinary boring life being shook up. But the reality was that she was scared and had absolutely no idea what was going to happen next.

As nice as it was that Anna had sent these men for her, Olivia realized she had noplace to go where she would be safe. But then Kirk tugged on her arm to keep her by his side, and she thought she was safe with him.

Chapter Eight

Kirk wasn't distracted by the woman. He kept a weather eye on their back trail as Laz maneuvered the car through the airport traffic. He heard a ragged sigh and glanced over at the woman.

She had a bruise on one cheek and her eyes were a bit wide. She started to talk, but he shook his head.

"Keep quiet."

Laz didn't need the distraction from his driving and Kirk wanted to concentrate on keeping her safe. The same concentration that had served him well on his last job came to the fore now.

Her breathing was loud and ragged and he spared another glance at her. She had her arms wrapped around her own waist and was rocking back and forth.

"Don't think about it," he said. "Try to picture something pleasant, one of your favorite things."

She nodded. He put on his shooting glasses. They looked like sunglasses and were good for reducing glare and sharpening images. There was someone in the car three behind them that he didn't trust.

"Watch that black Land Rover, Laz."

"I am. Can you read the plate?"

He could and did, giving the plate number using the phonetic alaphabet.

"Got it," Savage said. "We're running the plate now."

"Should we lose them?" Laz asked.

"Affirmative."

"Raindrops on roses," Olivia said.

"What the hell?" Kirk glanced over at her again.

Her face was white, pale white. She was in shock. Damn. "Stop singing."

She didn't pay attention to him. "Whiskers on kittens."

Laz was doing a good job of getting them through the traffic and away from the Land Rover.

"That car checks out," Savage said. "Find a safe area and get rid of everything that she has on her. Lambert's guards came after her, so that means he might have a GPS tracking system in her mobile phone."

"Will do, boss," Kirk said.

Laz consulted his GPS navigator and Savage said something else, but Kirk couldn't hear him over Olivia's singing.

"Shut up," he said, making his voice harsh and low.

She looked up at him with wide eyes. He wasn't being mean, just doing his job. They couldn't save her and keep her safe if they were distracted.

"Sorry . . . you said think of my favorite things," she said.

"Think, not sing."

Without warning, she started crying. He had dealt with men in the field before who'd lost it, but a woman . . . Why was she any different than men? He pinched the fleshy part of her upper arm.

She slapped his hand away and glared at him.

Thank God the tears had dried up.

"Why did you do that?" she asked.

"To make you stop crying."

"Oh. Thanks, I think."

He nodded.

"I found a neighborhood where we can dump her stuff. I think it might be better if she's not seen with us here," Laz said.

Kirk nodded. "Olivia, get down on the floor."

"Okay," she said. She curled her long legs under herself on the floorboards. He noticed her shiver first and realized shock was setting in. He was reaching down to rub her neck when she made a gagging noise and then threw up on his shoes.

"Sorry," she muttered.

"Laz, you got any water up there?"

Laz passed a bottle back. Kirk met Laz's eyes in the mirror and the other man lifted both eyebrows at him. He shrugged. In the course of his career he'd been bled on, vomited on, spit on—hell, there was hardly anything that hadn't landed on him at one time or another.

He poured some of the water on the napkin he took from his pocket and handed it to her. "Wipe your face."

She nodded and took it. Her hands were still shaking. "Do you think you are going to get sick again?"

"Not now," she said.

She wiped her face and he noticed how pale she was and how scared she looked.

"I'm so sorry," she said again, tears falling from the corners of her eyes. "Don't pinch me again."

"Then stop crying."

She blinked. "I'm trying. How do you do it?"

"Not cry?" he asked. He hadn't cried since Armand had died more than three years ago.

"No," she said, wiping her face delicately with the cloth he'd given her. "Not react to this kind of situation."

He shrugged. "It's what I do."

"That's not helpful."

"My job is to keep you alive, not give you advice."

"Are you good at your job?" she asked. He looked like he would excel at anything he put his mind to, but looks could be deceiving.

"Very."

She nodded at him. "I'm glad."

"We're here," Laz said. He'd pulled the car into a parking lot in a rough neighborhood.

"Sit tight," Kirk said, getting out of the car. He made sure the area was secure, then turned back to the Mercedes.

"Give me all of her stuff," he said.

"What?! What are you doing with it?"

"We're not sure that Lambert hasn't bugged your bag and phone."

Olivia started to argue, but he just glared at her. She closed her mouth. Her stuff wasn't going to keep her safe . . . only this man would.

"I need my BlackBerry. It has everything in there. And I took some files from Ray's desk."

"Get the files out. But you can't keep the phone," Kirk said.

He shook his head. He tossed her bag and then opened the back of her phone and took out her SIM card. He tossed the phone on top of her bag in the trash can and got back into the car.

"I . . ."

"Be quiet. Laz needs to concentrate."

"Anna wants to talk to Olivia," Savage said.

"She doesn't have a phone, so call mine."

"Will do," Savage said.

His cell phone rang. He checked the caller ID first and than handed it to Olivia.

"Who is it?"

"Anna."

She took it and held it to her chest as if it would offer her some kind of comfort. And he guessed that the comfort of having something normal in her hands was almost too much.

"Where are we headed, Jack?"

"The safe house in Pretoria. Laz has the directions. I might need you to go to the police department. You managed to avoid most of the surveillance cameras in the airport, but the ones in the hallway behind the restaurant recorded everything."

"Did you get a copy of it?" Kirk asked.

"Yes. You're covered. We need to debrief her."

"Will do."

"The rest of the team will be en route to Johannesburg shortly."

"Why? Laz and I have this covered. When are we extracting her?"

"We are waiting for approval from the South African government. They want to talk to Olivia about what she saw. Remember I called the cops in Cullinan."

"That's right. I'll debrief her and we can send them a report."

"After we get the information from Olivia, I'll put Laz on guard duty."

"Affirmative."

"Is everything okay?"

"Fine. I need to process the operation."

"Our clients were very happy. You got a bonus, by the way, for being neat and clean."

"Thanks." Kirk was always clean. He didn't see the need to kill anyone who wasn't a target. And he never had.

"At least this job should be neater."

"Doubtful," Kirk said.

"She threw up on him," Laz added.

Jack laughed. "That's a woman for you."

Kirk looked at the woman in question and found her looking up at him. Her eyes were wide and so damned blue he thought the Caribbean paled in comparison. There was a large bruise forming under her right eye.

One kill was affecting her a lot, he thought. And she'd only seen it from a distance . . . she was worlds too soft for this kind of action.

"Are you okay?" Anna asked.

No. She wasn't okay. An odd calm had come over her once they'd thrown out all her stuff. All her stuff, she thought. She had nothing but a pair of battered running shoes and this Chanel pantsuit.

"Fine. I'll call you when we get to wherever we are going," Olivia said.

"Kirk and Laz are the best. They won't let anyone get to you. I can't believe those men almost abducted you in the airport."

"Me, either. I should have realized that Ray would send Burati after me."

"No, you shouldn't have, I should have. I'm sorry about that, Ola. I figured I had you in a safe public place."

"I don't know that public places are safe now."

"They aren't," Kirk said. "But we'll get you to the house and take care of everything."

She glanced up at him. He made her feel like she could take a deep breath and just relax. It didn't matter that she was crouched on the floor in the backseat of a car still in Johannesburg. She knew that if she was with Kirk he wouldn't let anything happen to her.

"I'll talk to you later, Anna."

"Okay, bye."

She handed Kirk back his phone. "Are we almost to . . . where are we going?"

"A safe house in Pretoria."

"I lived in Sandton," she said, shivering at the thought of going back there. That *House Beautiful* home that she'd been so impressed with when she'd first seen it.

"You'll be safe with me," he said.

She believed him. He didn't seem like someone who made promises he couldn't keep.

"Who were those men who apprehended you? Did you know them?" Kirk asked.

She was close to losing it again as she remembered Burati's face. "Burati . . . the man who had me was my bodyguard. The other man, his name is Barack, I don't know him."

Kirk nodded. "Do you think your fiancé sent them after you?" Kirk asked. His voice was low and gravelly.

She pictured Ray's face as he'd aimed that gun at her car. The deadly intent in his eyes had chilled her then and continued to make her uneasy. Ray was definitely willing to kill her to keep his secrets safe.

"Yes, I do."

"The authorities in Cullinan are going to want to talk to you about that," Kirk asked. "When we get to the safe house in Pretoria I'll take your statement and we'll send it to them."

"I took a bunch of stuff from Ray's home office," she said.

"Why?"

"To be honest, I'm not sure. I just took everything that was in this locked drawer he had at home. Including a file he asked me to bring to him. Do you want to see it?"

Kirk nodded. "But not now. When we get to the safe house, I'm going to need you to go over every detail of what happened today. Do you think you can do that, tell me everything that happened?"

She nodded. As much as she wanted to forget everything

that had happened to her today, it was impossible to escape the details of it. Over and over in her head were the images of Ray and then the menace in Burati's eyes when he'd grabbed her at that restaurant. "I think Burati meant to kill me."

"Probably. He seemed like a pro to me."

"Anna is looking into his past to try to figure out what he did before he worked for Ray," Olivia said.

She shook her head. "I can't believe I'm having a conversation with you."

"Why not?" he asked.

"Well, fifteen minutes ago I was fighting for my life. This has been the strangest day." Olivia thought about her singing earlier and blushed. "Sorry for singing."

"It's okay."

"I'm not your usual client, am I?" she asked.

"No."

"What's your normal—"

"I'm not big on talking," Kirk said.

"Sorry," she said. She pulled her knees closer to her chest, resting her head on them. When she closed her eyes, it all came back to her. Ray leveling that gun at her. Burati grabbing her and dragging her from a café.

"How did you get here so quickly?" she asked.

"We were in Africa."

"Where?"

"North of here," Kirk said.

"Morocco? I love Rabat. They have some of the best little markets for shopping."

He shook his head and turned to stare out the window at the passing scenery.

But all she could see was his shoes covered in a towel and her own knees.

"Are you usually a bodyguard?" she asked him. She knew very little of what Anna did except that she worked for or used to work for Liberty Investigations. And that the work Anna did usually involved corporate crimes and stuff like that. This man didn't seem like the kind of guy who would blend in in the corporate world.

"Sometimes," he said.

"That was nice and vague," she said, finding a little of her equilibrium as they talked. She realized, crouched on the floor at his feet, that she was starting to get the distance she needed from Ray and everything that had happened. She was going to be okay.

"Our line of work isn't one that warrants discussion," he said.

Laz laughed. "That's the most politic answer I've ever heard you give."

"Shut it, Laz and keep your eyes on the road."

The other man chuckled one more time. "We work for whoever needs us."

"I can't imagine you in an office," she said to Kirk. He wore a pair of camouflage pants and a plain T-shirt that fit him like a second skin.

"I don't do office work. I'm a field agent."

"I can see that," she said. "You seem like someone more at home in the outdoors than in the concrete jungle." He was tan and had sun lines at the corner of his eyes. Whatever he did, a lot of his time was spent in the sun. She shook her head. He was a mercenary, she thought. She was having a conversation with a man who was a gun for hire.

"You are a very reassuring man," she said.

He gave her an odd look. She knew he wanted her to stop talking, but she found the more she talked the better she felt.

"I've never felt so scared before."

"Are you going to throw up again?" he asked, wryly.

She shook her head, then sighed and put her head down on her knees. She wanted to go back to bed and start this day over again, she thought. She didn't care that Ray was the kind of man he was, if she didn't know . . . wait a minute, she wasn't that type of girl. It was a good thing that she knew the truth.

She needed to make sure that Ray didn't kill anyone else. She couldn't believe she'd slept with a murderer.

That she'd shared her home and her body with a man who was capable not only of killing someone she didn't know but also of killing *her*. It made her queasy and she turned aside, not wanting to throw up again.

She started humming again. Strangely, that song was a comfort to her. Her favorite things were running flat out with nothing but her iPod buzzing in her ears. Dancing at midnight on New Year's Eve, she thought. Swimming in the Mediterranean on a crystal clear summer's day.

"You're singing again," he said.

"I'm sorry I keep wigging out. I guess you don't react to things like I do," she said. Then realized how stupid that was to say. This was a guy who had taken on two armed men to save her. Of course he wasn't bothered by violence and its aftereffects.

He seemed immune to everything. What if she could be like him? Honestly, if this became mundane to her she'd wonder if she had a soul left. Or if she'd simply stopped feeling. She was scared and angry and tired and achy.

A million other emotions were blended in with those feelings. She wanted to curl up somewhere and hide from the world and at the same time she wanted to find Ray and kick him really hard. Let him know that he might have scared her, but he hadn't really intimidated her.

She wasn't sure that last part was true, but she was going to pretend it was for now. That was really all that she could do. It was either that or break down and start crying and if she did that she was afraid she'd never stop.

Chapter Nine

Kirk kept a vigilant eye out as they drove through the afflu-ent suburb. This safe house was one they'd used before. He had a stash of weapons and clothes at the house, and he was looking forward to getting there.

The house had state-of-the-art security, including a safe room with video monitors where he could keep an eye on everything that was going on around them.

Once they were ensconced there he'd debrief Olivia, send that report to the local authorities, and then work on getting Savage to extract her. The only way Olivia was truly going to be safe was if she was away from Lambert and his henchmen.

The safe house was in a neighborhood near the one where Olivia lived, according to Anna, but Jack had thought hiding close to the enemy was a good idea. They entered the secured subdivision using the automatic gate key that had been left for them in an airport locker. Laz had picked it up when he'd got-ten the keys to this car.

The Savage Seven had safe houses all over the world and

the keys were left in airports and train stations. Savage was a big believer in being prepared and in contingency plans.

They entered the tree-lined neighborhood and Laz slowly pulled into the garage. Olivia made a move to get up, but Kirk pressed his hand to her shoulder to keep her in place.

This house seemed safe enough and there was no connection to Olivia to it for Lambert to exploit, but they never took chances. Safety was the first order of business where she was concerned.

"Stay here while Laz checks out the house," Kirk said.

"How long will he be?"

Kirk shrugged. Damn, this woman liked to talk.

The garage door closed behind them, enveloping them in the darkness of the garage once Laz killed the lights. He didn't turn on the garage light, instead leaving the area in darkness. That would give Kirk the advantage if anyone came into the garage from the house and not give away his position.

Laz got out and entered the house. Kirk left the window up and the doors locked. The vehicle had bulletproof windows, so from a safety standpoint, Olivia was good.

"I'm in," Laz said through the earpiece. "The place looks clean, but let me check all the rooms."

"Affirmative," Kirk said.

"Are you talking to me?" Olivia asked.

"No. I was talking to Laz."

"It's odd because I suspected that, but I was raised to respond when anyone speaks. I was also raised to marry a rich man. That may have been what led me into this mess."

Kirk realized that talking soothed her. He should make the effort to have a conversation with her, but that could lead to him being distracted and that was never a good idea.

"House is clean," Laz said in his earpiece.

"Affirmative."

"We're going to get out of the car now. I want you to let me

THE MERCENARY 63

get out first. Once I'm in position I will tell you to move. Just get out and walk toward the door."

"I can't see."

"Follow me," he said.

He got out of the car and kept his weapon drawn. Olivia stepped out and stood close to him. He felt her shivering as she put her hand on his arm.

There was a loud explosion sound. Kirk didn't hesitate to toss Olivia back into the car. He came down on top of her, prepared to protect her from the gunshots.

"Stay down," Laz said in his ear.

"What the fuck was that?"

"Checking it out now," Laz said.

Olivia was shaking even more.

"What—"

He put his hand over her mouth. "Quiet."

There wasn't another shot and nothing but the sound of a car driving down the street.

"Car backfire," Laz said. "You're clear."

Kirk pushed himself up and saw that Olivia was staring up at him. With his infrared glasses on, she was visible to him. He noticed she'd been crying again, but she'd kept quiet, and he had to respect that.

"Let's go."

She nodded, but didn't move even after he'd gotten off her.

She was going to lose it again, he thought. "Come on."

She sat up, but just kept her arms wrapped around her. "I'm . . . I don't think I've ever been this terrified before. Nothing is the way it should be."

He nodded.

"I want this to all go away," she said.

"It won't. It can't unless you die. And I'm not going to let that happen. Just get out of the car and you'll start to feel better."

She scooted across the seat and then stood up. "I still can't see."

"I can."

He took her hand and led her toward the door. But she didn't move.

"What now?"

"Thank you."

"For what?"

"Everything," she said. She came closer to him in the dimly lit garage. Going up on her tiptoes, she brushed her lips over his, lingering for just a second before she turned and went into the house.

Kirk was glad that Olivia went upstairs for a shower. Laz took a few minutes to access what they needed and then left to exchange their car, pick up supplies, and make sure that no one had followed them. Laz was also going to check the airport to see if Burati had returned there.

"Savage?"

"Here."

"I think we need to set up a more active perimeter while we have Olivia in the house. When you are in-country I'd recommend leaving Hamm at the guard gate."

"Do you think the safe house has been compromised?"

"No. But we don't know what we are dealing with yet."

"Agreed. I'll contact the security staff at the subdivision and let them know what we'll need."

"Can you get us a video patch from the guard gate? I'd like to monitor everyone in and out."

"Will do," Savage said.

"Anna got a call from Lambert at the D.C. number. We are going to downplay the connection there. It wouldn't take much digging to find out that she and I are married."

"Another reason to stay single," Kirk said.

"What? Wait until you fall for a woman—"

"Not happening. What do you know about the bodyguard?"

"Anna pulled a file on him. He grew up in Soweto."

"Lots of development going on there," Kirk said. "Lots of violence, too."

"Yes, there is. He has lost his father and two older brothers working at the Onyx Diamond Mines."

That was an interesting connection. "How? Is mining that dangerous?"

"I don't know that much about it, but I'm doing some research."

"Can Burati be made to work for us?" Kirk asked. The simplest way to eliminate the threat to Olivia was to get her out of the country, but since that wasn't an option, they had to either kill the men who were after her or bring them over to their side.

"I don't know the measure of him yet. I'm hoping to talk to him once we get to Johannesburg."

"When will that be?"

"Tomorrow. We are gathering supplies and getting the men ready. Anna is trying to contact Olivia's parents."

"I'm going to debrief her and then I'll send the report to you."

"Good. If you need anything else, just yell."

"I will. Mann out."

"Savage out."

Kirk paced around the house, making sure that the locks were secure and the connections on the windows and doors that activated the alarms were all sitting properly. Then he went back to the front room, which gave him the best view of the downstairs area.

He could cover the entrance to the garage and the front door from there. He also saw the stairs if he sat in the right spot. He checked his weapon and then found a quiet place on the floor to sit.

He found once he stilled his body he could hear more than the sounds near him. He could feel the vibrations of people and animals in the vicinity.

He sat quietly. He'd taken his shirt off because it was hot. He sank down into a cross-legged pose and put his gun on the floor in front of him. He opened his mind and let the night fall in around him.

He still had his earpiece in and monitored Laz's communications. But the other man was quiet now. He heard the shower shut off upstairs and hoped that Olivia had found a way to stem the tears that she'd battled on and off since he met her.

Olivia tried to have a shower, but she didn't feel safe and in the end had to settle for washing up in the sink. She knew it was ridiculous to place her faith in a man like Kirk, but then again maybe that was the smartest thing she'd done. He was the one person who'd kept her safe all day.

And it was too quiet downstairs. What if something had happened to Kirk and Laz? Anna had told her that they needed every detail she had on Ray to help figure out what had happened and how best to protect her.

Laz was going out to get supplies and change vehicles. Olivia was really impressed with the team that Kirk was a part of. And, to be honest, she was really impressed with Kirk. She cautioned herself that she might be feeling a bit of hero-worship where he was concerned, but she couldn't help that. He made her feel safe, and that was the only thing that mattered.

She ran down the stairs, anxious to not be alone anymore. The shadows in the house didn't scare her, but the shadows in her mind did.

Kirk was sitting in the dimly lit living room when she came

down the stairs. He had no shirt on and was sitting cross-legged on the floor facing the empty fireplace. She stood quietly on the threshold, wishing she could back away and leave him alone, but she was fascinated by this new side of the man she wanted to know more about.

"Sorry to disturb you," she said, walking into the room.

"What's up?" he asked as he turned to face her.

"Um . . ." How was she going to tell him that she just needed his company? This bristly man didn't seem to like having anyone around. "I—Anna said you needed some statements from me."

"I do," he said, getting to his feet.

Her stomach rumbled and he arched one eyebrow at her. Oh, my God, that was embarrassing.

"How's the stomach?"

"Fine. I'm a bit hungry. I don't know why, but I really want chicken-fried steak and mashed potatoes."

He shrugged. "Sometimes comfort foods are what you need after a scare like you had."

"Maybe that's it," she said. She hadn't eaten that meal since she'd turned thirteen and her father had transferred to the United Kingdom.

"What's your favorite meal?"

He shrugged, something she realized he did a lot. "Steak."

He wasn't going to say any more. His ways were simple and quiet. He wasn't a talker and she had to get used to it. "What were you doing just now?"

"Meditating."

"Really?"

"Yeah, I think there's a box of nuts in the kitchen. Wait here and I'll get them."

He walked out of the room and she followed him. She didn't want to be alone. Maybe later she'd be fine with it, but right now, she wasn't.

"I told you to wait."

"I don't take orders," she said.

"Maybe in your everyday life, but as long as you're under my protection you will."

"Fine, but I can't be alone right now."

"Why not?"

She shrugged.

He narrowed his eyes on her. "Don't clam up now."

"Sorry I talk too much."

"It's fine. What's with you not wanting to be alone?" he asked.

She didn't want to say that he'd somehow become her touchstone. She didn't want to tell him that she needed him.

"Olivia, talk to me."

It was funny, really. She'd wanted him to talk to her and he hadn't. But now that she was quiet he wanted words from her.

"I can't be alone right now. I'm scared."

He nodded, then went to the pantry and took out a can of dry roasted nuts and handed her a vitamin water. "Sit down over there. We'll get started on your debriefing."

"You've got kind eyes," she said.

"Kind eyes?"

"You're the kind of person who cares about strangers."

"Not really," he said.

She shivered. Was she putting her trust in the wrong man? The image of him coming into the hallway and rescuing her from Burati played in her mind. He was the only man she trusted.

"Sit down and get comfortable," he said. "I'm going to ask you a bunch of questions. I'll record everything you say."

"Okay."

"Before we get started, do you have the stuff you took from Lambert?"

"Yes. I left it upstairs. Should I go get it?" she asked.

"Yes, please."

She left the room but couldn't make herself go upstairs. It was dark and . . . suck it up, she thought. Was she really going to stand here like some kind of wimp? Kirk wasn't going to let anyone into the house or upstairs while she was there.

She took a deep breath and ran up the stairs two at a time. She held on to the railing and then ran flat out to the room she'd been given. She'd left the lights on and she entered the room quietly. She took the pile of things from the dresser and then ran back downstairs.

She hadn't had a chance to look at them and she hoped there was something incriminating in the information despite the fact that she was having a hard time believing the man who wooed her in London would want to kill her. Even though she'd seen him with the gun and he'd sent her bodyguard after her. She wondered if she'd simply misinterpreted things.

Kirk still sat where she'd left him. He'd turned on an overhead light now but had left his shirt off. She could see his skin better and realized he had a lot of scars on his back.

"What happened?"

"When?" he asked turning to glance over his shoulder at her.

She walked over and put her hand on his back and moved her fingers lightly over his skin, tracing the scars that covered his back.

"Fire," he said. Standing up, he walked over to his T-shirt and pulled it on.

"You didn't have to put your shirt on," she said.

"Yes, I did."

"I'm sorry if I made you uncomfortable," she said. She had

liked touching him. Had been wondering how he'd feel since the moment he'd come to her rescue. Well, to be honest, she hadn't thought of that until they'd been in the car together and she'd started feeling safe.

Her fascination had to stem from the fact that he wasn't like any other man she knew.

"I'm not uncomfortable," he said. "I just don't think it's a good idea for you to touch me."

"Why not?" she asked, because she thought after the way he'd touched her that he was interested in her. Oh, man, what if she was reaching for him because she needed the distraction? The distraction from her memories of today, from the betrayal that Ray had inflicted on her.

"You've just been through a traumatic event and you aren't yourself."

"What makes you sure?"

"I've been a woman's adrenaline lover before."

"What a rude thing to say," she said. She wasn't going to pretend that she hadn't been looking at him in a sexual way, but it was more than that. The attraction she felt for him stemmed from . . . she didn't know what it stemmed from.

"Just calling it like I see it," he said. He walked back over to her and tipped her head up toward his. "I don't want you to regret anything, Olivia."

There it was again—the way he touched her. "I can live with the consequences of my actions."

"Can you?"

"Yes," she said. Then to prove that she could, she went up on tiptoe and kissed him.

Kirk pulled Olivia more fully into his arms, tilting his head to the side and opening his mouth over hers. She held on to his shoulders as he kissed her.

He had wanted to do this since the moment he'd looked into those big wide blue eyes of hers. And now that he had her in his arms, he wasn't in a hurry to let her go or to rush this kiss.

She was a woman to be savored, and that was exactly what he did. He swept his hands over her delicate shoulders and down her shoulder blades, simply enjoying the womanly feel of her in his arms.

His meditation had been for hell. All he'd concentrated on was her. She was a distraction and that was the one thing he couldn't afford. Distracted men were dead, and Kirk hadn't survived as long as he had by doing stupid things like picturing her in the shower naked. Imagining her soapy hands moving slowly over her body. He had been half tempted to go up the stairs and wait for her in her bedroom, but he'd resisted.

Ha! Barely. And now here he was with her mouth under his and her silky body pressed close to his, but not close enough. The layers of clothing separating their bodies frustrated him.

He slid his hand under the hem of her blouse just at her waist and felt her skin. It was what he'd wanted and she shifted in his arms, saying his name on a sigh. He kissed her again, sucking her lower lip into his mouth to taste her.

"What are you doing?"

"Stopping."

"Why?"

"Because I'm on duty right now. And keeping you safe is more important than . . . anything else."

She nodded. "Thank you. I think I'm afraid of being alone."

"I'm here."

She bit her lower lip and then looked up at him. "Promise?"

"Yes. Now where is the stuff you took from Lambert's desk?"

She bent over and picked up the papers and files off the

floor. "Here it is. It might be nothing, but he had it locked up and hid the key so I think it must be important to him."

"I'd reckon it is. I'm not going to pretend I know what any of this stuff is, but we have a guy on our team who can put everything in the computer and make sense of it."

"That's great. I think I can help with this," she said, pulling a small leather wallet from the pile.

"What is it?"

"An account book for a Swiss bank account. I didn't know he had a Swiss accountant," she said.

"There seems to be a lot about that man you didn't know."

"You're right. The hard part is adjusting to the fact that the man I was about to marry could betray me so deeply."

"Don't take it personally," Kirk said. Olivia didn't strike him as the kind of woman that a man would betray. Not normally, so he could only suspect that Ray Lambert had always led two lives and he had asked Olivia to marry him to legitimatize his second life.

"I guess so. I mean I didn't know much about him beyond what he told me. I'm sorry about kissing you the way I did when I came downstairs," she said. "I needed to forget and . . ."

"Don't worry about it," he said, sifting through the papers on the table.

A sheen of tears appeared in her eyes. "I just don't feel safe anymore. I've always had this innate belief that things were going to work out and now that's gone and I don't know how to cope. It's not fair of me to lean on you this way, but I don't know what else to do."

"Trust me," he said.

She was shaking and on the verge of losing it again. If it had been anyone else he would have walked away and let her deal with it on her own, but this woman was different.

He pulled her into his arms and offered the comfort of a

hug. He hoped the strength of his body—the body he'd honed to a lethal edge for killing—could offer her more than just some reassurance. He wanted her to understand he wasn't going to let anything happen to her. He didn't understand it, but he knew it was important to him that Olivia made it out of this mess alive and with her sense of security restored.

Chapter Ten

AUGUST 1, ONYX DIAMOND MINES, CULLINAN

Ray wasn't the kind of man who dealt with incompetence well. When he was called to the police office to pick up Burati and his accomplice, it was all he could do to keep his tone civil.

"I'm sure it was a misunderstanding with my fiancée. She was panicked by living in this city with all the security that's needed."

"I understand, sir," police officer Monroe said.

"Do you have any information on the man who took her?"

"Nothing as of yet. We are going over the security footage from the airport and hope we will be able to identify him soon."

"Very good. Are my men free to go?"

"Yes, Mr. Lambert."

Ray walked out of the police station with Burati and his hired man behind him. He waited until Nels opened the door for him and they were seated in the back of his limousine before he reached over and slapped Burati.

"What the hell were you thinking?"

"I'm sorry, sir. I never expected anyone to be following her."

Ray shook with rage. This entire situation was getting out of control. "I need this taken care of. Did you recognize the man who took her?"

"No, but she asked him a question," Burati said.

"What question?"

"Give me a minute . . . Kirk? I think that's the name she called him by. Does she know anyone by that name?" Burati asked.

"I don't know. We will go through her computer files when we get back to the house."

"Yes, sir."

"Did she ever meet a man while I was at work?"

"No. This man isn't from your circle. He was rough and a hired killer."

"How would she know someone who was a hired killer?" Ray asked.

Burati didn't say anything and Ray let his mind wander. "She didn't book a ticket, either, so she lied to me."

"She didn't have a lot of time at the airport," Burati said.

"About an hour and a half after she left the house. I want a man to watch the airport. If she shows up there, I want to know about it."

"I will do it myself, sir."

"No, not you. Someone else. I need you to try to identify the man who took her."

Burati nodded.

They drove through the darkening night of Johannesburg. Ray felt impotent with anger. He wanted to shake Olivia and mete out some kind of pain to her for the problems she was causing him.

He doubted she even realized that she had information that

could cripple him. Those files she stole held more than just his private bank accounts; they also held his personal network of black-market contacts and details of every deal he'd done. It was the kind of information that the diamond consortium would use to fire him from the mines and probably have him prosecuted and sent to jail for the rest of his life if they didn't decide to make a lot of trouble for him and probably kill him.

Ray rubbed the back of his neck. How could one little woman cause so much trouble?

They pulled into the garage and Ray got out, leaving the security guards to do what he'd asked them to. He went into his office and sat down, logging on to his PC so he could do a few searches of Olivia's computer. When she'd come to live here he'd had his computer guy from the mines come out and rig up a home network.

He'd also had him add a shadow drive on Olivia's computer so he'd know what she did. The first thing he did was open her e-mail account.

While that loaded, he looked at the picture of her on his desk. It had been taken in London. They'd had dinner at the British Museum and in the background of the photo you could see Big Ben.

He'd always felt like things weren't going to work out between the two of them. He had believed the problems were class differences, because Olivia was every inch the lady and he was nothing more than a lad from Jo'burg who'd worked his way up the corporate ladder.

But being betrayed by her this way really pissed him off. He picked up the frame and threw it against the wall, unable to look at her smiling face one more minute.

The smashing of the glass as the frame broke apart was satisfying. So was the thought that he would find Olivia and she would pay for what she'd done to him.

He wasn't a man who tolerated betrayal—something she'd

learn soon enough. He picked up his cell phone and called Burati.

"Where are you?"

"In my office, sir. I have a message in to the police department. I have a friend who works in counterterrorism. He's going to send over some mug-shot books for me to search through."

"Good job," Ray said. Burati might not be the idiot he'd proved to be this afternoon. "I want Olivia brought to me alive when you find her. I want to question her before you kill her."

"Yes, sir."

He disconnected the call and started searching her files. There was no mention of anyone named Kirk in the e-mails. Most of her friends were as shallow as she was.

Who was it she had said she was going to visit? Someone in D.C. Ray remembered. He typed in D.C. and found Anna Sterling . . . at libertyinvestigations.com. That didn't seem like one of the normal bubbleheaded heiresses who made up Olivia's circle of friends.

Burati was ready to quit. And he called Phillip to let him know that.

"This is Phillip."

"Burati here. I didn't get Olivia. Someone else took her. At first I thought it might have been a man hired by Lambert, but it wasn't. I have no idea who has her."

"I'll work on finding out through my contacts," Phillip said. "I believe it was your brother who was killed, Burati."

"Me, too," Burati said. It had been a long day and he was aching and tired and frustrated.

"I'm ready to quit," Burati said.

"Don't give up. We will get Lambert, but only with your help."

"Everything should have been over by now."

"Indeed it should have, but we'll get him yet."

"I know we will. We're going through mug-shot books from the local police to try to identify the men who took Olivia. And I believe that Lambert is going to announce her kidnapping to the media."

"I suggested that course of action."

"I did my best to keep her safe," Burati said. His hand ached and was bleeding. He'd been bandaged, but he didn't like getting shot at.

"I know you did. Olivia has a classmate who is a private investigator and bodyguard," Phillip said. "Anna Sterling, she may be contacting you."

"That's not a good idea," Burati said. "Lambert is already tracking that connection. It might be less complicated if I stay hidden for now."

"I agree," Phillip said after a few minutes. "I'm going to need you to go through Lambert's office one night."

"Tonight?"

"No, Burati. Take the night to grieve for your brother. Is there anything I can do for you?"

"Just make sure that Lambert doesn't kill any more of my kin."

"That's my goal."

"Then we're good," Burati said, hanging up the phone. He worked on identifying the man who'd taken Olivia Pontuf from his office at the Lambert house, but his heart was filled with sad thoughts of his brother and the young life that had been cut short.

Burati didn't like the man he was becoming as he kept working for both Lambert and Phillip. He did like the idea of the man he'd be once he only worked for Phillip. And he also pictured himself going back to his ghetto in Soweto and building houses, real houses with cement walls instead of cardboard ones.

Chapter Eleven

Olivia sat between Laz and Kirk as they ate a supper of fast food. Neither man said much; they just sat and ate tensely. She knew they were there on duty guarding her and she wanted to say it made her feel safer but honestly nothing could.

The picture they were putting together of Ray Lambert scared her. In the file they'd gone through was an account of seven men who'd been killed by Ray. All of them had been part of his illegal operation. Ray was not the man she thought she knew.

"I can't believe Ray would be selling diamonds on the side. The consortium is very protective of what goes out to the market," Olivia said.

Kirk shrugged. He ate the French fries three at a time and she watched the methodical way he ate his food. She realized he ate for energy and not for pleasure.

She was scarfing down the fries like nobody's business. A part of her realized she was eating because—well, because she could control that.

"Why would he do that?" Olivia asked. "He makes a very good salary, so it's not like he needs the money. And he doesn't live that extravagantly. He didn't even offer me an allowance."

Kirk put his burger down and looked over at her, obviously guessing she wasn't going to stop talking. She wanted to sit quietly like these men both were, but she couldn't. The silence was grating on her already raw nerves.

"Who knows?" Kirk asked.

"Everyone always needs a little more money," Laz said. "I know I'd like a little extra so I can trick out my boat."

"Really?" she asked. "What kind of boat is it?"

"It's a nice little speedboat, but I'd like a cabin cruiser," Laz said.

She tipped her head to the side. "I'm having a hard time picturing either of you in a normal life. How do you go home from a job like this?"

Kirk shrugged. Olivia rolled her eyes. "It wouldn't hurt you to answer a question."

He leaned forward, looking her straight in the eye. "My job is to protect you until the threat to you has passed. How is talking going to help that?"

Laz didn't come to her defense or tell him to lighten up.

"Sorry. I'm going a little crazy and I need something normal. Talking helps me forget."

Laz didn't say anything, but Kirk nodded. "I don't talk about my downtime."

"Why do you think Ray would turn to crime?" she asked, after a few minutes had gone by.

"We see people who do all kinds of things for money. He might have an addiction to drugs you don't know about."

"It's not drugs," Olivia said. "I lost one of my friends to an overdose when we were in college. I know what that kind of addiction looks like."

"Women, gambling. It doesn't matter what he's addicted to, just that he needs money to pay for it," Laz said.

"I never saw any signs of that stuff," she said. "But I didn't pay close attention. We had a whirlwind courtship, and until I moved here a little over a month ago we lived separate lives. I can't think straight."

"That's understandable," Laz said. "I remember the first time I saw a man killed. I puked up my guts."

"That's a nice image, Laz," Kirk said. "You might want to watch your mouth while we're eating."

"Sorry."

There was such calmness in these men that it was helping Olivia relax. She really needed to do that, because deep inside she kept feeling that insidious panic working its way closer to the surface.

"I don't know why he needed me to bring this information out to him," she said, pulling the papers from the black envelope. They'd been over the papers a couple of times. There were names and numbers—but not phone numbers—in there, and also the names of the men he'd killed. Why would he need that at the mines?

Neither man said anything.

"Anna is going to run those names through the computer and see what she can find. But these numbers look like something specific. I wonder if it's related to the raw diamonds that he was selling or maybe a location where they were taken from or the carat weight."

"Who knows?" Laz asked. "Is there anything in that notebook?"

She pulled the thin wire-bound notebook that had been in one of the file folders closer. She opened it up and there were numbers in similar patterns in there, but until they knew what it meant it was all gibberish.

"I'm not much good at this sort of thing," Laz said. "Getting transportation in the middle of nowhere, that I can do, but this stuff—nah."

"Me, too," Olivia said. "I know I'm not an expert, but working to figure this out makes me feel productive."

Kirk just kept eating.

"I'm going to take a walk around the perimeter and catch some shut-eye," Laz said.

"Go on," Kirk said. "I'll wake you at midnight."

"Sounds good."

Laz left the room and she watched him go. "He's a good guy."

Kirk didn't say anything. She wondered if she should just give up on getting him to talk. But she couldn't. It didn't bother her when Laz left her alone, but she had been terrified when Kirk had.

"How long have you worked with him?" she asked.

"A while," he said.

She turned around to face him. "You specialize in vague answers, do you know that?"

He shrugged.

"I want to know more about you and your team," she said.

"Why?"

To make sense of who he was. "Just so I know. Who do you work for?"

"Right now—you."

"Great, then if you work for me I want some answers."

"My team is called the Savage Seven. We are mercenaries."

She wrinkled her nose. She had no idea what mercenaries were really like. Hired guns to be certain, but Laz and Kirk didn't seem like conscienceless monsters. "What does it mean to be a mercenary?"

"We work for whoever hires us."

It was the most he'd revealed about himself and she ate it

up, wanting to know more about Kirk Mann. "And there are seven of you?"

"There were. Armand died on a mission in Morocco a few years ago."

"I'm so sorry. I guess that was hard on you guys?"

"Very. We haven't replaced him . . . well, I don't think we ever could. Armand was a big part of the team and each of us really took his death hard."

"What happened?" Olivia asked. She couldn't imagine a group of men making a mistake that would lead to the death of one of their own. Laz and Kirk had given her the impression that they were more competent than that.

"We were betrayed. We found the leak and plugged it, but it was too late to save Armand. We vowed to never let that happen again, and we haven't."

"How can you make sure it doesn't happen again?" she asked.

"By being very picky about who we trust and who we work for."

He walked away from her and she realized that she had been picking at his past and she hadn't wanted that. She'd simply wanted to understand this complex man.

Kirk didn't like talking. *Period.* There was something about Olivia that made him want to ease her fears. But he was trying to ignore it.

"Why are you still in this business?" she asked.

He'd forgotten she was still sitting next to him. How he'd done that, he had no idea, because she smelled so sweet and tempting he'd had a hard time concentrating on going over the papers she'd brought. But he was a professional and he wasn't going to take a chance with her safety.

His mind was fried from the first job he'd pulled this morning. Was it only this morning? It felt like a lifetime ago. He needed to regroup because Olivia was rattling him. This itty-bitty girl he could bench-press was winding him up—making him feel things that he hadn't in a long time.

Things like sympathy. She was trying so damned hard to act normal and pretend that her life was going to be the same. All the while, he wanted to warn her it never would be again.

"Kirk?"

"I'm still in the business because I'm not trained to do anything else."

"But it must take a toll on you."

"Not really. It's just a job," he said. Then looked at her. She held her hands tightly laced together and watched him with wide eyes. She was going to start crying or singing again, and he couldn't handle either one of those.

"So. You're a writer?"

She leaned forward. "Yes. I am. I love it. It's such a fun thing to do. It's a big adventure to make my life seem a little bit out of the ordinary."

"I bet your life doesn't feel ordinary now," he said.

"No, it doesn't. Is your life like that? Is this normal for you?" she asked.

He shrugged. "My job with our team is one that I've trained myself to do."

"How do you become a mercenary?" she asked.

"I was a Marine sniper before I came to work for the Savage Seven."

"I can't imagine being able to do your job."

Very few men could do his job and fewer women. It was pride that made him confident of that. Distancing himself from his humanity had been his only saving grace. The only way he could continue to do his job and still survive.

"What are we going to do now?" she asked pulling her hand away from him.

"Wait for Savage to get here."

"Do you have a plan?"

"Keep you alive."

She gave him a sarcastic smile. "Shouldn't we set a trap and catch Ray?"

"How?"

"I don't know . . . maybe I could call him and offer to give him back his stuff if he calls off his guard dogs. Then we can set up a trap for him and capture him."

Kirk didn't say anything.

"Is that not a good idea?" she asked.

He didn't know. His job was to protect her for right now. When Savage got here, he could go in and figure out what the best solution to the Lambert problem was. If that meant killing him, then Kirk would take the shot.

"Maybe I should call the police," she said. "Or mention my plans to them when I talk to them tomorrow about the murder I witnessed."

"The local cops' hands are tied because the murder you witnessed happened on diamond mine property and they are a law unto themselves," he said.

"This is more complicated that I ever imagined it was. Ray's not going to just let me disappear, is he?"

"Not until you're dead or he's in jail. He's not going to rest until he gets this information back and can be assured you aren't going to talk to anyone about what you know."

She wrapped her arms around her waist. "To think my biggest worry before this was if my marrying Ray was going to be too boring."

Kirk said nothing to that. He glanced at her hands and realized she wasn't wearing an engagement ring.

"You're staring at my ring finger," she said.

He scratched his head. "I was wondering about your fiancé."

"What about him?" she asked. "He never gave me a ring. I'm not really into big jewels. I know that seems counter to everything else I stand for, but I'm not a fussy person."

"I was thinking that it must have pissed you off to realize that your soon-to-be-husband tried to have you killed."

"I don't get pissed," she said. "It scared me."

"Because he waved a gun at you?"

"Yes." She stood up and stretched. "I'm tired, but I don't know if I can sleep."

"I will be on duty; no one will get to you while you sleep."

"I don't know if that will be enough to help," she said.

"I'm on guard duty until midnight." He wondered if she was getting tired but didn't know how to tell him she wanted to leave. What if she had guessed that he liked her and she was staying just to make him feel better?

"I'll sit up with you," she said softly. "Unless you want to be alone."

"I do," he said. He doubted he'd be a decent guard with her by his side. He sent her up to her room and set about patrolling the empty house. Olivia was awake with her lights on and each time he passed her room she called out to him.

Kirk just kept walking and focused on his job. At midnight Laz relieved him and he went upstairs to catch a few Zs in one of the bedrooms.

Olivia had left her door open. She was lying on the bed fully dressed, with a book in her lap.

Olivia didn't have any pajamas with her, something that was distressing to her. But then she figured she wasn't going to sleep. Kirk walked by her room several times and finally she realized that he was still here and he was watching over her. She got a book from the shelf, a biography of Nelson Mandela. She started to read it, but drifted off to sleep.

Olivia woke up and got out of bed. She walked down the stairs when she heard a noise. She got to the bottom of the stairs and Burati was waiting for her. He had a gun in his hand and held it aimed at her head.

"Come here, Ms. Olivia."

She shook her head and turned to run. But Ray was behind her. How had he gotten behind her?

"Now, Olivia, that's not very polite," he said.

She screamed.

Bolting upright in bed, she couldn't stop shaking.

Kirk appeared in the doorway with his gun in one hand. He scanned the room and then looked at her.

"I'm sorry."

"She's fine. Just a dream," Kirk said.

It took her a minute to realize he was talking to Laz on their wireless earpieces.

He walked into her room and crossed to the bathroom. He appeared a minute later with a glass of water.

He handed it to her and she sipped at it. There was no way a drink of water was going to make her feel better.

The aftereffects of her day were getting to her. She hoped at some point she'd be able to use these feelings constructively, but right now she was simply tired and overwhelmed.

She looked up from her water.

Kirk stood there. He was big, tall, and almost scary-looking in the dim light provided by her bedside lamp. But to her he was a welcome sight.

Kirk Mann had come to represent her security. It was funny because Pretoria had fences and guards and she felt safe with Kirk. Something she'd never felt with Ray.

He tipped his head to the side watching her. "Are you comfortable sleeping in your clothes?"

"No, I'm not."

"I'll get a T-shirt for you," he said.

It was the first time he'd reached out to do something for

her. Something that wasn't saving her life. And she knew that his job was to keep her safe and that was what he was doing, but this small kindest melted her.

She waited, hardly breathing, until he returned. He handed her a big black cotton T-shirt that was obviously well-worn. She took it from him.

"Thank you."

This new person she'd become after being attacked was vulnerable and needy in a way the old Olivia had never been.

He started to leave, but she knew she couldn't sleep without him. "Kirk?"

"Yeah?"

"Will you stay in here?"

He nodded.

She didn't give him a chance to change his mind. She rushed into the bathroom and changed out of her designer pantsuit into the T-shirt he'd loaned her. It was big, dwarfing her body, and made her feel . . . safe. Just the way Kirk did.

He wasn't in the room when she came out and she was disappointed, thinking he'd left. She climbed into the bed, hearing the squeak of the bedsprings. A minute later Kirk appeared in the doorway.

He had his handgun tucked into the waistband of his jeans. She noticed he had his wireless communicator in his ear. He was her protector, this gun for hire, and she realized that her own worldview had changed.

Just yesterday she would have said that guns for hire were wrong, that a man who'd sell his loyalty was a step above a criminal. Today her view had changed. Today she realized that he was . . . her hero. Why did she keep coming back to that?

No man had ever been a hero to her before. No man had ever cared enough to do this. Even her own father had simply asked her nanny to stay in the room with her when she'd been younger and afraid.

Suddenly she felt very silly asking him to stay. "You don't have to be here if you don't want to."

He shook his head. He walked into the room and put his gun on her nightstand. She looked at the weapon. It was sleek and smooth, and she had no doubt he knew how to use it. She'd seen that this man was more than a guard; he'd been a weapon in that hallway, efficient and deadly as he had saved her from Ray's men.

He was probably sick of her being a clinging vine.

"You want me to be stronger tomorrow."

"Of course I do," he said, sounding a bit impatient with her conclusion.

"I'm sorry if I've been . . . a bother."

"You saw something horrific," he said. "It's understand-able."

She closed her eyes and then opened them back up again. Kirk still stood above her bed. He was watching her carefully, and she realized what she'd thought was annoyance might be a little bit of caring.

"I don't think one night is going to be enough to make me feel safe again."

"Its not, but it will do a world of good to start you in the right direction."

She nodded, knowing he was right. He glanced around and then went across the room to the chair by the window. He dragged it over one-handed and she watched the flex and play of his muscles as he drew the chair across the room. He angled it near her bed so that he was close.

"Go to sleep."

She raised one eyebrow at him. "It's not that easy."

"Why not?"

"It takes me a while to fall asleep," she said. It always had. When she was a little girl, before her parents had sent her to boarding school, her maid used to sit in a chair next to her bed until Olivia drifted off to sleep. "Can you just go to sleep on command?"

"Yes."

"Of course you can, you're G.I. Joe."

He almost smiled and that comforted her the way his big soft T-shirt did.

"Close your eyes," he said.

She closed them again, but when she did she saw Burati's face as he'd bound her hands. Saw the knowledge in his eyes that he was going to kill her. She jerked upright and opened her eyes.

"What is it?"

"I keep seeing Burati."

"Ah, baby, I'm sorry."

Baby. He'd called her baby, she thought. Later that would be significant to her. When she had time to think about the fact that this man who was used to protecting others had called her an endearment. She knew it meant something to him and that made her feel special.

"Will you hold my hand until I go to sleep?" she asked.

He held his big hand out to her and she reached for it, letting his hand engulf hers. He held her hand perfectly again but soon her arm was tingling from the odd angle and she wondered if she'd get any sleep tonight. He reached over and turned off the light.

"Kirk?" Her voice was soft, almost a whisper, as if she were afraid to wake him up.

"Hmm?"

"Will you hold me?"

He hesitated.

"I'm sorry, but you did say you'd keep me safe and right now my dreams—rather nightmares—are threatening me."

"Fine."

He got onto the bed with her, careful to stay on top of the covers.

And as she curled on her side and wrapped her arm around his waist and felt his arm around her shoulder she knew that it was Kirk Mann she wanted. Not any other man but this tough man who made her feel safe.

Chapter Twelve

Ray smiled genially as he entered his office and found Lars and Phillip from the diamond consortium waiting for him. Anita had called him on the way in to let him know the other men had been in the office when she'd arrived.

He'd been on the phone with Phillip since Olivia's disappearance. Both men were concerned about her and Ray hadn't had to fake the fact that he had no idea what had happened to his fiancée.

He had called Lars and Phillip yesterday to let them know that he'd found one of his employees stealing rough diamonds and had let them know he'd dealt with Thomas. While the consortium would never publicly okay killing, Ray realized that they were pleased he'd plugged that gap.

"Good morning, gentleman. Has Anita taken care of everything you needed until I got here?"

"Good morning, Lambert. Yes, your assistant has been very helpful," Lars said. He was a tall blond man and spoke with a South African accent. This mine had been his before he'd earned a spot on the consortium and Ray knew that Lars still took a personal interest in this mine.

"Good. What can I do for you gentlemen?"

"We want to see the mining operation so we can determine how long Thomas was stealing from us. Then we need to see your production logs," Phillip said.

Phillip was a dark-haired aristocrat who'd grown up in Great Britain. He and Olivia had travelled in the same circle of friends and it had been through Phillip that he'd met her at a family birthday party for Phillip's mother-in-law.

Ray couldn't breathe for a minute as the ramifications of everything started to weigh down on him. He reminded himself that he was much smarter than these two men. He'd out-witted them for the last seven years without them having a clue as to what he'd been doing.

He wasn't about to let it all go to hell now.

"No problem. Our logs are kept in the conference room down the hall. Why don't we go down there and take a look at them? I have the stones I took off Thomas yesterday. I have already determined the part of the mine he took them from and we can tour that after we are finished with the logs."

He led the way down to the conference room. His cell phone beeped and he glanced at the unit to see he had a text message from Burati. "Will you give me a moment, gentlemen?"

"Yes. But please don't be long. We want to talk to you as we go over the logs."

"Of course. I'll send my assistant down to take notes as we go over everything."

He walked back into the office. "Go take notes, Anita. They are going to have a lot of questions."

"Yes, sir."

"Were they here when you arrived?" he asked Anita. The

woman was efficient and usually guarded his office like a mother hen with her last chick.

"Yes. They were in your office."

"In my files?"

"I don't know. When I walked into my office Lars came out." She stood up. "Would you like me to go through the files and see what is missing?"

"Thank you, Anita."

He entered his own office and closed the door. He'd left the photo of Olivia on his desk here. Figured it'd be a good idea to keep everything that involved her as if she were just missing. Speaking of his missing fiancée . . . he called Burati.

"What did you find out about her friend Anna?" he asked as soon as the other man answered his phone.

"Anna Sterling is a private investigator. Near as I can tell, Liberty Investigations does work for corporations—usually white-collar crimes. The Web site information is very vague and everyone I've contacted says little is known about them. I left messages wherever I could for them to call us."

This was why he'd hired Burati in the first place. The man was a top-notch investigator and a really good guard. "Great. Have you found out who the man was who took Olivia?"

"No. That is proving harder to do. I'm still looking through photos and searching Internet databases," Burati paused. "Ms. Pontuf's mother called this morning, sir."

"I should have called them sooner, but to be honest I didn't think of this angle. I think we should tell her parents she's been kidnapped. While I'm calling them, I want you to notify the police that she was taken."

"Yes, sir."

Ray made a note to call Olivia's parents. "I will call her parents. Maybe some publicity will generate a few leads. But in the meantime I want you to keep looking for her."

"We know they left the airport so they might still be in Jo'Burg."

"Or anywhere in South Africa. Do you have contacts in Cape Town?" Ray said. He wanted to delegate this entire matter to Burati but didn't know if he could trust this man with the delicate operation if Ray didn't keep overseeing him.

"Yes, I do know some people down in Cape Town. I will send Ms. Pontuf's picture to everyone I know in the area."

"Very good. Keep me posted."

He hung up from his call to Burati and dialed Olivia's parents house. Their maid answered. "I need to speak to Mrs. Pontuf. This is Ray Lambert."

"She is at breakfast this morning, sir. May I take a message?"

"Have her call me as soon as possible. Please tell her that there is an emergency involving her daughter."

"Very well, sir."

His office door opened as he disconnected the call with the maid. Phillip stood there. "We need you."

"Sorry, Phillip," Ray said. "I've been trying to reach Olivia's parents, because I thought they should be the first to know that Olivia has been kidnapped."

"Good idea. I wanted to wait until we were alone to discuss the details. What happened yesterday?" Phillip asked.

"Her bodyguard was attacked at the airport and she was taken by a man that no one has been able to identify."

"Do you think she was taken in retaliation by the men Thomas worked for?" Phillip asked.

"That would be my guess," Ray said, realizing that Olivia might still be of use to him. "But it would only be a guess, Phillip."

"We need to get our security force on this. We still have questions about the logs, but right now finding Olivia might give us more information. Have you spoken to the police?"

"Yes, they are looking through their international criminal database to try to identify the man who took her."

"They have a photo of him? How is that possible?"

"She was taken at the airport," Ray said. "The man grabbed her from a café while she was waiting for her flight."

"Where was she going? Back to London?" Phillip asked.

"She said she was going to visit a school chum in the States."

The rest of the morning was spent searching for Olivia, and Ray felt like he was back in control. Things couldn't have been going better if he'd planned it this way.

Olivia showered and dressed and came out to an empty bedroom, but she'd expected that. Kirk had said he needed to get back on guard duty and relieve Laz. She turned on the radio as she got dressed in yesterday's clothes. She dropped her brush as she heard news of her kidnapping on the radio.

She sat on the bed as she listened to the announcer telling listeners that she'd been taken against her will at the airport. They said that no ransom had been demanded yet.

"Oh my God," she said. She had no makeup and there wasn't any in the bathroom. She looked at her face in the mirror. She was very pale. She was vulnerable without Kirk by her side. She slicked her wet hair back into a ponytail and went downstairs.

"Have you heard the news broadcast?" she asked Laz when she entered the kitchen. He leaned against the counter holding a cup of coffee in one hand and eating a piece of toast.

"Yes, the alert just came on. How did you know about the news?"

"It's on the radio. Is it on the television as well?" she asked. All of her friends here . . . okay, she didn't have that many, but they'd be worried about her.

"Yes. They have a grainy picture of Kirk leading you out of

the airport," Laz said. "But it will be very hard for anyone to identify him as your kidnapper."

She sat down in one of the kitchen chairs. "I have to call my parents."

"No," Kirk said entering the room. He looked good to her in his T-shirt and khaki pants. "That will give you away. They will accuse you of stealing from Ray."

"Why?"

"Because they say that you were carrying some important papers for the Onyx Diamond Group and suspect your kidnapping has something to do with that."

"This is a big mess. My parents are going to be upset."

"Of course," Laz said. "But we need to do the best we can to keep them safe. Do you think that Lambert knows you went willingly with Kirk?"

"Yes, I know he does. Burati heard me call you by name." Olivia wished she'd kept quiet, but to be fair it had been her first kidnapping and rescue. And she suspected that it took some time to get used to doing the right thing under pressure.

"Damn," Kirk said. "Savage wants a conference call in ten minutes."

"Can I come, too?" Olivia said.

Kirk hadn't said a word about last night and she realized he probably wasn't going to. She'd thought that today would have to be better than yesterday, but now she wasn't sure. Kirk was treating her like a stranger, the world thought she'd been kidnapped, and her parents would be going nuts once they got word. Today seemed to be another crazy day. And she wondered if her life would ever get back to normal.

Laz led the way out of the kitchen. She realized he wasn't distant, just prudent. He wasn't going to let anything get in the way of saving her. And that was kind of reassuring, but she wasn't sure she liked the way he could switch off his emotions.

She couldn't do that and all she really wanted was to be in

his arms, to feel his strength wrapped around her so she'd have the sense that she was safe. Because seeing her photo on the television didn't make her feel safe at all.

They kept playing the grainy airport image and her engagement announcement photo. "Why didn't I realize Ray would do this?"

"How could you know?" Kirk asked. "We thought he'd come after you."

"He still will," Laz said. "Only when he kills you he's going to blame Kirk."

She flushed and felt faint at the thought of dying. She hugged herself even tighter than she had before. What had she been thinking last night? There was no safety for her in this new life she'd stumbled into.

Kirk put both hands on her shoulders. "You aren't going to die, Olivia."

She shook her head. Only Kirk could protect her until they were able to get Ray behind bars. And even then she might not be safe. And what would happen if he got her parents?

"Look at me," he said. There was such command in his voice. So much confidence and she wasn't sure of anything at all. She was just a little coward who kept getting more scared with each hour that went by.

"Olivia?"

She shook her head. She was barely holding it together. If he looked at her with either annoyance or pity she'd lose it.

"Laz, will you give us a minute?" she asked.

Laz left the room. She walked over to Kirk and put her arms around him. He hesitated and then wrapped his arms around her. "I'm scared."

"I know."

"You make me feel safe."

"Good." He tried to step away, but she held him close. She needed this.

"Tell me what you are afraid of," he said.

"I'm scared for my parents. Ray could kill them."

"We won't let that happen. Lambert isn't going to get away with this. We are going to stop him and keep you and your family safe."

"How?" she asked.

"Anna will call your parents. They know her, right?"

"Yes," she said. "They do. I'm sorry for breaking down a bit."

"That's understandable. The first time I saw an image of myself on the news as a murderer it shook me."

"Murderer?"

"I have been accused of some hairy stuff. I've done some things that might not make you feel comfortable, but those things—my skills—are the only thing that can keep you safe now."

She swallowed hard. She had pushed the reality of what being a mercenary meant. Had tried to ignore the fact that a man with scars from gunshots and knife wounds and burns wasn't a man who'd lived a safe life. He would have had to do things that were unimaginable to her.

"I'm better now. You are the best man to keep me safe, and I'm very glad to be here with you."

Kirk said nothing else, simply let her go. Olivia walked away from him, trying to think only about this moment and not beyond it. That wasn't too hard considering she had no idea what the future held for her.

Every neat little plan she'd made was now in the past and she was starting from scratch and learning about herself again in the process.

Burati called Phillip as soon as he was done alerting the media to the fact that Olivia Pontuf had been kidnapped.

"I can only talk for a moment," Phillip said.

"That's fine. I haven't gotten any closer to finding Olivia. Lambert asked me to notify the media that she has been kidnapped and I did."

"Good. Please keep me informed of any information you get. Do you have someone you can trust who works with you?" Phillip asked.

"I can get Barack again. Why?"

"I want to set up a bug here in Lambert's office and I'd also like to have some photos taken of the files in the secretary's office. He moved some of them before we were able to read them.

"I can do that. When do you want me to do this?"

"Soon. I will let you know when we can be sure that Lambert won't be in. I'm almost to the mine so I'll have to let you go for now. Thanks for the call."

"You're welcome," Burati said.

He hung up and called his cousin to tell him that he'd pay him well for one night's work. He warned the other man that they wouldn't have a lot of notice. Barack was used to doing work when asked and had no problem with it.

Kirk didn't like the way Lambert had played this latest bit of information, but he did admire the man. He was smart and they had to take that into account when they were dealing with him. Olivia had left the room and he let her go earlier because there was nothing he could say to change her mind about the man he was.

And he didn't apologize for who he was. He simply wouldn't because he knew he was a necessary evil.

"Anna is on the phone with the Pontufs. They are very concerned about their daughter and are not sure who to trust. We are lucky that they know Anna. Is Olivia on the line?" Savage asked.

"No," Kirk said. He'd sent her out of the room and told her

to go lie down and rest. He needed some time away from her. She was distracting him. Last night when he'd held her in his arms, he'd realized just how much he'd enjoyed it. And that was something he couldn't afford to let happen now.

"Just Laz and I. Do you need her?"

"In a minute. We aren't going to let them know that you are working for us. I think the less they know the better. Lambert had already called them before Anna did, so we don't want to tell them anything that will change their attitude toward him and possibly put their lives in danger."

"Have you thought about asking Charity or Justine to come to Johannesburg and serve as bodyguards for them?" Kirk asked. Charity and Justine were coworkers of Anna's at Liberty Investigations. The firm was a top-rated investigation and security firm. The three women worked together like a well-oiled machine. Having worked with them in the past, Kirk was very impressed with the three of them. Those women could kick some serious ass.

"We have. Charity is on her way. Justine will be coming in the next day or so. She'll help us to gather information to put Lambert in jail," Jack said.

"Good. I want this wrapped up as soon as we can. Olivia's not going to last too long in this kind of environment," Kirk said.

"I think we can wrap this up in three or four days tops. Do either of you have any contacts with the diamond consortium?"

"I don't," Kirk said.

"I might," Laz said. "Let me see what I can come up with. That is a hard nut to crack. They are very particular about who gets into that organization."

"I know. I've been online and on the phone trying to find someone we can use on the inside, but I haven't gotten very far," Savage said.

"We might have to just use Anna and Charity on the inside with the Pontufs. That will be enough to get us some information on whatever Lambert has planned. Olivia managed to get some information that will implicate him in the black-market diamond exchange. I'm sure his bosses at the consortium don't know about that."

"Good idea," Savage said. "Let's move forward with that. Get a package of information together that Charity can use if she has the opportunity."

"We will," Kirk said. "When will you be in-country?"

"Six hours. We are landing at a private airfield. Do you think we should get Olivia out of the country?" Jack asked.

"No. I can keep her safer here."

"I wouldn't go anyway," Olivia said coming back into the room. She had a bottle of water in one hand and looked very calm and untouchable.

"Why not?" Savage asked.

"My parents are on their way here and Ray is dangerous. I couldn't possibly stay someplace safe while they were in peril."

"Glad to hear you feel that way, Olivia. I'm Jack Savage, by the way."

"Nice to talk to you. Thank you for sending your men after me."

"It was nothing. They were in the area anyway."

"Doing what?" she asked. "Never mind. I probably don't need to know. Did Kirk tell you that we have a list of men we think that Ray killed? As well as a log of some sort to different areas of the mine that he was using for his illegal mining?"

"I did," Kirk said.

"We don't have a diamond expert on our team. Are you familiar with that operation, Olivia?" Savage asked.

"Not really. I can make a guess at some of the things that are in the book, but I don't really know what any of it means. I have a cousin who works at the diamond consortium, but I probably shouldn't call him now, should I?"

"No, that wouldn't be a good idea. We will figure that out. Why don't you and Kirk keep trying to figure out the logs until we get there?"

"We can do that," Kirk said. "Laz and I want to take a drive by Lambert's house to see what the security setup is."

"Wait until the rest of the team is in Johannesburg," Jack said. "Your face is on that tape and I don't want to take a chance of you being recognized."

"I was going to shave my head," Kirk said.

"Why would you do that?" Olivia asked.

"It'll change my look. I can let my beard grow in and dress like a Muslim, too. That might be a better disguise," Kirk said.

"Whichever you decide. You're good at keeping out of sight. I'll talk to you both later unless you need anything else?" Jack asked.

"We're good," Kirk said. He hung up the speakerphone and jotted a few notes on the paper he'd been writing on.

"How often have you done something like that?"

"Like what?" he asked, not really sure what she was asking.

"Cut your hair or grown your beard. Pretended to be someone of a different religion . . . actually, I don't know what religion you are," she said.

He could see that she was starting to panic about not really knowing him.

"Who are you?"

"Whomever I need to be to get the job done," he said, walking away from her.

That was something he'd learned a long time ago being a mercenary. And it was one thing he'd never forget.

Chapter Thirteen

Olivia followed Kirk out of the living room and up the stairs. She wasn't sure where he was going, but she wasn't prepared to stay by herself.

"Stop following me," Kirk said without turning around.

"I . . . I don't want to be alone."

"I'm going to work out."

"Good. I could use some exercise," she said. "I'm used to running every day. Burati used to hate going with me."

"Fine."

She climbed the stairs behind him and followed him into a sophisticated workout room. "This house has everything."

"It should. We need a home base to minimize our running around in a town when we land."

"Do you have many of them?"

"A fair amount. You'll find running shorts and T-shirts in the closet. I'm going to my room to change."

"Uh."

"You will be fine for a minute."

She nodded. She got changed quickly and went back in the

exercise room. The treadmill was one she was familiar with and she went to it. She put her hands on the handbar and felt a sense of the normal for a second. Looking around this room she could be anywhere: London, Manhattan, Paris. In this room she was safe.

He came back out dressed in athletic shorts and no shirt. He had on tennis shoes and held an MP3 player in his left hand.

"Why don't you stock this place for women?" she asked. There was a lot of Kirk's mercenary world she simply didn't understand and it was only by asking questions that she'd come closer to getting it. That she'd come closer to figuring out what it was about Kirk Mann that made him so irresistible to her.

"There aren't any women on our team and we don't usually have anyone here who isn't on the team."

She went into the bathroom and got changed. Running would actually help to make her feel normal, she thought, though she was no longer sure what normal was. She had realized while listening to Kirk and Jack talk that her life was never going to be the same again. She couldn't go back to pretending she didn't know that men like Kirk existed.

She'd learned more about him since they'd met yesterday than she knew about Ray in all the months they'd been engaged. That was a lie. She didn't know Kirk, and that was fine because the one thing she did know about him—he was very good at keeping her safe—was the only thing that mattered right now. She tried to imagine the future and not feeling this vulnerable, but she couldn't.

The most important thing to her way of thinking was the fact that Kirk wouldn't lie to her the way Ray had. He wasn't the type of man to smile at her one day and try to kill her the next.

Kirk was already running on the treadmill. She watched

him run, admiring the athleticism of his body. She fiddled with the settings until she got it set to her stride and pace and started running. She didn't have headphones, so she just let her mind wander and found that she was able to start making some sense of the events of yesterday.

Well, as much sense as she could. She thought that Ray must have killed a man who either had threatened to go to the authorities about his illegal activities or a man who was doing illegal work for him. She didn't know that man, but she offered a quick prayer for him.

Why had Ray called her to bring the black envelope to him? The file in there had made no sense to her or to Laz or Kirk when they'd all looked at it.

Maybe someone else on the Savage Seven would be able to figure it out. The information seemed to be about a defunct shaft of the mine. In fact, the pages were all about the mines that had been abandoned at one time or another. She tried to remember the conversations she'd had with Phillip at a dinner party last year. She knew that the consortium routinely ordered the different mines to shut down to keep control over output. She kept jogging, letting the cadence of her feet center her.

What if that defunct mining shaft was where Ray was mining his illegal gems?

She hit the stop button and turned to look at Kirk, who was still running, sweat trickling down his back. She reached over to trace the track of it down the center of his spine.

He hit the stop button and turned to her. His breath was heavy and his chest was moving up and down. She realized she wanted him. How was that possible? She had never had much of a libido before him, but it seemed the adrenaline from her brush with death was manifesting itself sexually.

* * *

Kirk was having a hard time keeping his hands to himself and his thoughts off Olivia. It took all of his willpower not to stop the treadmill, grab her, pull her down on the floor in the gym, and make love to her.

It felt like eons since he'd felt the soft touch of a woman and he wanted Olivia's silky legs wrapped around his hips.

"What?" he asked her. His voice was rough with desire and he didn't bother trying to disguise the hard-on pressing against his shorts.

"Um . . . I was thinking that the information in that black envelope." She seemed a bit distracted by his body. Her eyes kept moving over his chest and she was running her thumb over her fingertips.

"What about it?" he asked, trying to get his mind back on track.

"What if he used the abandoned mine for his illegal activities?" she asked.

Kirk stepped off the treadmill and away from Olivia. She looked tempting in that baggy T-shirt with the sweat mark in the center. The baggy shorts just served to emphasis the slimness of her waist and hips.

Lambert, he thought. He had to keep his mind on Lambert. The sooner they got this girl back to her safe little world the sooner he could be back to normal.

"That makes a lot of sense. I bet he is using it," Kirk said.

"That's the only way he'd be able to get the diamonds he's selling on the black market. The consortium is very tight about what is mined. They won't allow the diamonds to be flooded onto the markets because that would erode their profits," she added.

"Let's go find a computer and see if we can see the mine from the satellite," Kirk said.

"Okay. I don't think it's available on regular satellites."

"We have access to government satellites, so we'll be able

to check it out. When do they do most of the mining at Onyx?"

Olivia bit her lip. "I don't know for sure. Ray would never let me come down for a tour. He works long hours like most businessmen."

"Let's get this information processed and see what it yields. Maybe we can go out and check out the mines," Kirk said.

He was tired of being in the house. He didn't like inactivity and though they'd only been here for less than twenty-four hours, he was restless. "You can stay here."

"No. I can't. You can't go alone and I don't think I can stay by myself."

Kirk rubbed the back of his neck "We'll figure something out."

He still couldn't get into Lambert's mind. And he had always been able to understand the men he targeted or the enemies he went after. One of the things he was good about was figuring out what made the other guy tick.

"Do you know anything about his past?"

She shrugged. "A little. His parents are deceased and he's an only child. Is that what you mean?"

"Yes. Where was he born?"

Olivia followed him down the stairs and he could feel her behind him. He was trying to ignore the lust for her, but it was hard because of her proximity. His hormones didn't rule him—at least not at this moment.

"I don't really know. I think he was raised here. I do know that he started working for Onyx and moved up the corporate ladder there."

"Has he only worked for them?" Kirk asked, building the picture of the man in his head. He should have done this earlier. But he had been too busy making sure she was safe. Now it was time to figure out Lambert and close this case.

"Yes. The mines are like that. Most people work for them

their entire life. In fact, there are generations of families who have always worked there."

"Even during different regimes?" he asked.

"Yes, they say that life doesn't really change for the poor," she said.

"That's true of any country. I've seen it everywhere I've travelled."

"Me, too," she said. "It's funny to me how people will hate someone of a different ethnic background without even realizing that they are basically the same. We all want the same things from life."

"You think?"

She nodded. "People just want to do the best for their families and keep them safe. Don't you think that's true?"

Kirk looked at her. "Probably. It's how we define 'best' that sets cultures apart."

"Yes, that's it. I have met people who were happy living in their dirt-floored huts in the Amazon. Happy because they had water and their kids had food. I mean that was literally enough for them to be happy."

They'd arrived in the living room and he leaned over the computer to wake it from sleep mode. He didn't want to think about how much he liked Olivia.

But somehow that didn't matter just now. Just now they were two people who were very much the same. They were two adults in an impossible situation, he thought. He wanted her and he needed to keep her safe. Would it be better to bed her and ease the ache inside or keep ignoring her?

He hadn't had a partner since his sniper scout Joe Gibbs had been killed on maneuvers. And he hadn't missed having one. He'd gotten used to working on his own and relying on his own skills and those of the Savage Seven.

Now this woman was making him remember things he'd forgotten, like how good it felt to share a discovery on a mission with someone else. And how much he enjoyed watching her butt as she walked.

This simple extraction was getting complicated and Kirk didn't like speed bumps on missions. He had to figure out what to do about Olivia and move on. Keeping her safe and out of harm's way was imperative. But shutting down Lambert and making sure that he didn't kill anyone else—especially Olivia—was his objective.

Olivia knew her way around the computer pretty well, but Kirk was better. He accessed a network that she didn't ask too many questions about and started searching for information on the mines that Onyx Diamond Group owned. It didn't take too long to find the proof that Ray was indeed mining in an abandoned area.

"I'm going to see if I can find satellite images of the murder you witnessed. Call Savage on this number and put him on speakerphone," Kirk said.

Olivia pulled a chair up to the table he was using and dialed the number on the satellite phone. "Savage here."

"It's Olivia. I'm going to put you on speaker," she said.

She pushed the button and set the phone on the table. "What's up?" Jack asked.

"Olivia made a connection to an abandoned area of the mine and I've been going over some of the satellite footage of the mine. There is definite activity there. I am also going to search for the murder she witnessed. Have you already done that?"

"Anna ran the time through the satellites that we have access to that would have been in that area and she didn't find anything," Jack said.

"So don't waste my time?"

"She's better than anyone I've seen on the computer." Savage's wife Anna was a computer whiz.

"I agree. I've made a digital copy of the activity I observed and I'm putting that in the file for Charity," Kirk said.

"Olivia, how well do you know that guy at the consortium?" Jack asked.

"I know him very well. He's married to one of my cousins." She had always liked Phillip—he was funny and charming and threw the best parties.

"Who is it, by the way?"

"Phillip Michaels."

"Do you trust him?" Jack asked.

"I think so," Olivia said. She'd never had any reason not to.

"Make damned sure you do, because you will be trusting him with your life," Kirk said.

That took her aback. For a minute, she'd felt like her old self again. But there was no going back to the old Olivia. Trust was second nature to her. She simply trusted everyone and she realized now that wasn't the best way to be. That, right now, if she put her faith in the wrong person it could mean her own death.

"He introduced me to Ray, but I don't think he knew about Ray's illegal activities," she said.

"You have to be positive. If you can trust him, then we can get Charity to go to him with the information we gather and that will help us to trap Lambert," Jack said.

"I'm not sure," she said. "I don't want to put Charity in danger. I mean, Phillip is one of the nicest men I know, but I would have said the same of Ray a few days ago."

"I will provide cover for Charity," Kirk said.

"What kind of cover?" she asked.

"Backup with my weapon," Kirk said. "But don't worry about that now. I wanted to let you know what we'd found."

"Thanks," Jack said. "I'm going to have Sam Liberty call the diamond consortium and see if he can get a lead on someone we can use. He has more contacts in that area than we do."

"Sounds good. Mann out," Kirk said, hanging up the phone.

"Who is Sam?"

"He owns Liberty Investigations. I've never met him, but Jack and he communicate on some of the jobs we've done. Sam works with a lot of governments and Fortune 500 companies, so he's got contacts everywhere."

"Do you think it's safe to leave this house?" she asked, thinking that maybe they could go and get her address book. She might have more information in there.

"Why?"

"Because I think if I got my address book I'd be able to find some of Ray's contacts."

"How will that help us?"

"Maybe someone has seen something."

Kirk shook his head. "We're not investigating this crime."

She nodded.

"I do want to go to his office. Is that where he spends most of his time?"

"Yes. Why?"

"I want to set up some bugs for recording. I think we need to find out what Ray is doing and who he is talking to."

"Okay. When will you go?"

"Soon."

"Are you thinking of leaving me here?"

"Not sure yet. If I take you with us, you'd have to stay well back and listen to orders. And no talking."

She nodded. "I think I'd prefer anything to sitting here worrying about Ray killing my parents or my friend. I hate this. I might not be a soldier like you are, but there must be something I can do."

"There is. Keep thinking like Ray," Kirk said. He really admired her guts and the way she wanted to do the right thing.

She was brave and willing to stand up for her family. That kind of loyalty meant a lot in his book.

"Well, I wouldn't have guessed he'd go public with my kidnapping, but I guess that makes sense. He can't take the blame for it. I bet the other guy he killed is going to take the fall for his illegal activities," she said.

"I'll make sure that doesn't happen," Kirk said.

"Why?"

"If it does, you'll never be free. You'll be the only one alive who knows his secret," Kirk said.

"You know it, too," she said.

But a smart man like Ray would suspect that Olivia would tell him everything, so he'd be searching for the two of them.

"We need to make sure he doesn't find out who I am," Kirk said.

"Why?"

"Because I have a long list of aliases, Olivia, and if he finds out who I am, it's going to make it impossible for you to be believed as anything other than a villain and maybe even the mastermind behind his illegal activities."

She backed away from him. "Who are you?"

"You know who I am," he said. And that was the truth. With her, he was a man with a soul. A man with a conscience. A man with hope for a life that might be lived beyond this job that had been his world for too long.

"The one man who makes me feel safe," she said.

Chapter Fourteen

Olivia tried not to dwell on the fact that Kirk was the man who made her feel safe. Instead she concentrated on the plan they'd laid out. She had a rough script that she was going to use to contact Phillip. Her cousin was the only one on the inside of the diamond consortium she could turn to. And she realized she was putting not just herself in danger but Kirk, Laz, and Anna.

Charity Keone had arrived early this morning and she looked like no bodyguard or private investigator that Olivia had ever seen. She had long blond hair and stood almost six feet tall. She was stunningly beautiful but she carried herself with the same kind of quiet confidence that Kirk did.

She wore a pantsuit and a shoulder holster for her handgun. Olivia had spent most of the morning just sitting quietly and listening to Kirk, Laz, and Charity talk about the situation. Olivia had answered questions when she'd been called on to, but for the most part she'd let her mind dwell on Kirk.

She was becoming obsessed with him. Last night she'd sat up until he'd come upstairs and asked him once again to sit in her room while she slept. He didn't argue and she'd found it comforting to have him so close once again.

"Olivia?"

"I'm sorry, I wasn't listening," she said.

"Your parents are making arrangements to leave their cruise and come to the city to help look for you according to Ray. I've contacted him and told him that I will be providing protection for your parents."

"Can you protect them?" Olivia asked. "If not, please just tell them to stay away. I don't want them in danger because— because I made the decision to trust the wrong man."

Charity nodded. "I am very good at what I do, and I promise you, your parents will be safe with me."

"Good," she said. Kirk gave her an odd look, which she ignored for now. "What do you need from me?"

"Things would go a lot easier if we had someone on the inside of the diamond consortium working with us."

"I can call Phillip," she said.

"Do you trust him?" Kirk asked. It was the first time he'd spoken to her since she'd told him he made her feel safe.

"Yes, of course I do."

"With your life?" Kirk asked again. "If you're wrong—well, that kind of mistake could be lethal."

She trusted Phillip but this situation was different. Would Phillip betray her? What if he was working with Ray?

"I have no idea if I can trust him with my life—with your lives. He's a cousin by marriage and he's always been kind to me."

Charity put her hand over Olivia's. "Then call him. If he's not trustworthy, I can handle him."

She looked over at Kirk and he nodded at her. She took a deep breath before dialing his number.

"This is Phillip."

"It's Olivia. Are you alone?"

"Olivia! My God. Are you okay? We are all so worried about you."

"I'm—I'm not too sure what I am. But for right now I am safe," she said, looking up at Kirk.

He just nodded at her. They had used a sophisticated phone that was untraceable, so there was no way that Phillip would be able to find her unless she set up a meeting with him.

"Good. Now what is going on? Do you need me to send a car to get you?" he asked.

"No. Ray tried to have me killed Phillip. I witnessed him killing another man. I am . . ." losing it, she thought. And she was. She was hyperventilating just remembering everything that had happened.

Kirk put his hand on her shoulder, and she glanced up at him feeling safe once again. "Are you shocked by what I've said?" she asked Ray.

"No, I'm not. We have been investigating Ray for a while now," Phillip said. "I'm sorry I didn't say anything to you but I never thought you were in danger from him."

"It's fine. I wouldn't have believed you if you had said something," Olivia said. She didn't want to dwell on the past or try to assign blame. She knew that she'd made a mistake by falling for a man she hardly knew. As she glanced over at Kirk, she warned herself not to do it again.

"Anyway, Phillip," she said before he could continue to apologize for introducing her to Ray, "I have a friend who works in the security sector and she has provided me with a bodyguard. Another person on her team is going to start investigating the murder with the cops. I had hoped that you would be able to work with us. To help us catch Ray and put him away."

"Who is this? You know that diamond consortium business is private. We handle our own problems," Phillip said.

Olivia felt a twinge of anger. "Well, this isn't private any more. He tried to kill me, and he is a threat to my parents. I don't think he's going to let me live, Phillip. He can't. I'm the one person who has seen him kill—the one person who can put him away for life, and he knows it."

"Yes, he does. Listen, I can't talk here. I have a meeting at Onyx in thirty minutes. Do you think you can meet me?"

Olivia put her hand over the mouthpiece of the phone. "Should I meet him?"

Kirk's first instinct was to say no. He didn't care about catching Ray Lambert and taking the man to jail. He cared about keeping Olivia safe and he couldn't do that if she was out of this house.

"I think that's a good idea," Charity said.

"It's crazy. It could be a trap."

"That's why you will be our secret weapon. No one is better at providing cover than you are," Charity said.

"I agree," Laz said.

"So yes?" Olivia asked.

Kirk realized she was looking at him. She was waiting for him to make the decision. "Yes, but you tell him where to come to meet us."

"Here?" she asked.

"No," Kirk and Laz said at the same time.

"Where?" she asked.

"My place," Charity said. "I'm staying in a condo near the business district. Give him my address."

She glanced at him again and Kirk nodded. The condo would be easy to control access to. And they'd be able to cover Phillip and anyone else who entered the building.

"I will meet you, Phillip," Olivia said.

She nodded and they set the time for later this afternoon. Kirk left the room while she finished up her conversation. He needed to get ready to be the sniper he was.

He needed his weapon and he needed to research the locale. He walked to the panic room, which had monitors, and—hell, it had everything he'd need. Laz was two steps behind him.

"I'm going to go over early and check out the security force that's already in place," Laz said.

"Take Charity with you. I'm going to suit Olivia up with a bulletproof vest and I'll bring her over with me."

"Sounds good. I'll send you images as soon as I have them. Do you think this is a trap?"

"I don't care. We're good with springing traps."

Laz laughed. "Hell, yes we are. Savage wants to talk to us both before this goes down."

Kirk pulled his cell phone out of his pocket and dialed Savage's number.

He put the phone on speaker just as Savage picked up.

"Savage here."

"We've set up a meeting with the diamond consortium and Olivia," Kirk said, then brought Savage up to speed on where they stood.

"Good. What's the plan?"

"I'm going over to case the building and check out existing security measures," Laz said. "Charity is going with me. The condo belongs to her husband, so we're not expecting too many issues."

"Good," Savage said. "Mann?"

"I'll bring Olivia and protect her until she's back in the safe house."

"Sounds like you boys don't even need me."

"Well, now that you mentioned it . . ."

The men all laughed, and Kirk recognized it for what it was. A way to blow off steam before a hairy mission. And this one had too many variables not to be hairy. He knew that Laz would secure the condo and an assailant would have to kill him to get to Olivia. But that still didn't mean this was going to be a cakewalk. Some of the must fucked-up situations he'd been in had started out as routine.

"Keep me posted," Savage said.

"What's your ETA?"

"Late tonight probably two a.m. We got held up in Germany, some problem with our plane."

"Fixed now?" Laz asked.

"Yes, we're good."

They ended the call with Savage just as there was a knock on the door.

Kirk walked over and opened it to find Olivia standing there. "Charity is on the phone with her boss."

Kirk had realized yesterday that Olivia felt safer with him. Hell, she'd *said* he was the man who made her feel safe. That was good. He could keep her safe as long as she kept her distance. As long as she remembered that he was her bodyguard and not anything else.

"I need you to get changed," Kirk said.

"I don't have any other clothes except your T-shirt."

Kirk led her out of the panic room and into the living area, where a shopping bag sat on the floor. "I think this is for you. Go upstairs and get changed."

"I . . ."

He arched one eyebrow at her when she stopped talking.

"I don't feel safe by myself."

"I'm right here, Olivia. No one is going to get by me."

She nodded. "Did I make you uncomfortable when I said you made me feel safe?"

He shook his head. "I'm damn good at my job. You should feel safe."

She bit her lower lip. "It's more than just you doing your job."

"No, it's not. This isn't your reality, Olivia. Whatever you are feeling is just your mind's way of getting you through this ordeal. Once you have your life back—you'll feel differently."

She didn't say another word, just turned on her heel and climbed the stairs. He watched her go, wishing for once he was wrong, but he knew he wasn't. He had never been wrong about this type of situation. And he knew that wishing wasn't useful.

Burati wasn't getting very far with finding the man who'd taken Olivia, and to be honest, that didn't bother him as much as it probably should have. He just needed to make sure that he kept the problem from getting worse.

He laughed out loud at the thought. What he had to do was keep Ray Lambert from killing Olivia. And that was going to be harder than it sounded. After all, Mr. Lambert was used to killing, and there were times when Burati believed that Lambert may have become addicted to it.

"Any news?" Lambert asked as he walked into the security room at his house.

"Nothing yet, sir. I have all of my contacts working on finding her."

"Good. Her parents are on their way here, and I want to have something to tell them. I am meeting with the police later today," Lambert said. "And I'd like to have a name or something to give them so they'll leave me alone about the thief I had to kill at the mines."

The thief? Burati clenched his fist to keep from punching Ray Lambert smack in the nose. His brother had been mourned quietly by their family last night, and Burati knew that putting Lambert in jail wasn't going to be enough.

Why didn't he simply shoot the man now?

Phillip would have him arrested, Burati thought. Killing Ray Lambert would mean he would be in jail. And Burati didn't want that.

"Did you hear me? I need a name."

Lambert's veneer of civilized sophistication was fading.

"Yes, I heard you, sir. I'm doing my best."

"Do better," Lambert said before turning on his heel and leaving. "Nels!"

"Yes, Mr. Ray."

"I'm ready to go to the mines."

A few minutes later, Burati was alone in the house and he sat back in his chair. He had been going over books of mug shots, but no one in them matched the man who'd taken Olivia. Burati realized that the man was probably a professional.

So he tried to focus on bone structure and eyes as he looked over the pictures. He knew he'd never forget the deadly intent in the eyes of the man who had taken Olivia from him.

His phone rang and he glanced at the caller ID. Phillip.

"This is Burati," he said.

"Phillip here. How was the service for your brother last night? I'm sorry I couldn't be there—did you get the flowers I sent?"

"Yes, we did. Thank you. What can I do for you this morning?"

Burati wasn't interested in talking too much about Thomas or his death. He wanted to focus on the future and on getting Ray Lambert in jail—that was the only way that was going to be able to truly put the past to rest.

"I had an interesting call this morning. It was from Olivia. She says she is fine and she wants to talk to me about setting a trap for Ray."

"Do you know who she is with?"

"She wouldn't say. I am going to meet with her this afternoon. I will mention that I have a man working on the inside. She has hired a bodyguard for her parents. A woman named Charity Keone-Williams."

"I think she works with Anna Sterling. I did some research into the Liberty Investigations group for Lambert."

Burati was glad to hear that Olivia had hired a guard for her parents. Lambert was getting desperate as his operation kept coming under scrutiny, and there was no telling what a desperate man would do.

Olivia was scared.

It was stupid, really, given the fact that she'd spent a lot of time in this part of Jo'burg. It was a place she'd visited and she had even attended a dinner party in this very condo building.

But everything here had changed.

She had changed, she realized. She wasn't the same person she had been before. She couldn't just walk into a room and not realize that she wasn't as safe as she'd thought she was. Not anymore.

Her thoughts were not productive, and she knew that she needed to stay focused. She was wearing a bulletproof vest under her clothing. Things couldn't get much more serious than this.

A bulletproof vest. She started shaking. Oh no, she thought. Now wasn't the time for a panic attack.

She needed to think. She needed to get her mind off her own fears.

She started humming, and just as she was about to start singing, Kirk reached over and put his hand on her thigh, squeezing tight.

"Sorry."

"It's okay. I just don't want to be distracted by your singing."

"I'm so sorry. I just feel like I'm going to crack into a million pieces."

He said nothing else, just concentrated on driving, and his calmness slowly seeped into her. He had taken his hand back but she reached over to put her own hand on his thigh.

He pulled into the underground garage and parked the car near the elevator.

"We're here."

"I can see that," she said.

"I was speaking to Laz."

"Oh."

He didn't turn the car off or make any move to get out. She sat quietly next to him.

"Okay, let's go."

He shut off the engine and undid his seatbelt. She did the same.

"I will come around and get your door."

He did and when she got out she realized that he was in full-on bodyguard mode. He kept scanning the interior of the garage and moved her quickly toward the elevator. But when she reached for the call button he knocked her hand down.

"We're taking the stairs."

"Why?"

"It's easier to set a trap for someone on an elevator," Kirk said.

He entered the stairwell before and scanned the area with his gun drawn. "We're in the stairwell and heading up."

"Laz again?"

"Yes. Just keep quiet and follow me."

"Yes, sir," she said, saluting smartly.

He stopped on the landing and turned to face her, crowding her back against the wall and using his body to protect her on all sides. "This isn't a joke."

"I know that," she said, hearing her own voice crack. "Believe me, I am well aware of the fact that I could die. That this trip out of the safe house could be my last."

Kirk rubbed his hand over the side of her face and leaned in as close as he could. "This isn't going to be your last trip, baby."

He turned his head and his lips brushed hers briefly before he started up the stairs again. She followed him. For the first time she thought that Kirk might be attracted to her as well.

Kirk wasn't a talker and he kept his feelings bottled up, but when he did communicate with her—well, then she felt like she'd found something very special. Something that almost made this entire situation worth it.

Because she'd searched for the kind of man that Kirk was for her entire adult life. He might not realize it, but his quiet brand of heroism was exactly what made him a man she didn't want to let slip away.

And she knew he'd say it was the situation, and that this wasn't the real world, but that didn't matter to her. She'd found a man who could keep her safe, and that was really all that mattered to her.

The meeting with Phillip went well. He had already been working on setting a trap for Ray and apologized again for not alerting her to his suspicions about Ray before she became his fiancée. Olivia doubted she would have believed Phillip or anyone else if they'd said that Ray wasn't the man she thought he was. She'd been a different woman then.

Charity and Phillip did most of the talking. Kirk stayed by the door, and Laz was in the security room watching all the monitors. They left the building thirty minutes later after a plan had been worked out. It had been decided that Olivia would stay hidden and Charity would approach Ray.

She'd tell him she'd been hired by Olivia's parents and try

to find information to incriminate him. That was fine with Olivia.

She wanted to get back to the safe house, where she knew nothing could happen to her. It wasn't that she didn't think that Kirk would protect her out here—she knew he could—it was simply that she wanted them both to be safe.

Chapter Fifteen

The team arrived that afternoon and Kirk spent his time locked away with Jack Savage and the other members of the team. Laz was the only familiar face, but even he seemed a bit scary when seen with the entire team—Jacob "Van" Donovan, the team's computer expert, "Wenz" Wenzel, the team's medic, and Hammond "Hamm" McIntyre.

"How are you holding up?" Anna asked.

They were sitting in the kitchen nook drinking a cup of tea. It was exactly what she'd needed and she was grateful to Anna for suggesting it.

"I'm doing okay," she said. She was, most of the time. She had no idea how she'd handle sleeping tonight, but that was later. She'd realized the only thing she could do was handle one thing at a time. Live in the moment.

"How were Mann and Laz?" Anna asked. "They are a little rough around the edges."

"They were fine. I feel so safe with Kirk."

"Kirk, is it?"

Olivia shrugged, then realized she'd picked up his habits.

But she didn't want to discuss how she felt about him. She had no idea where the intense feelings she had for him came from—she only knew they were there.

"Did you say someone had talked to my parents?" Olivia asked.

"Yes, I did. Charity Keone, a woman who works with me, is going to work with them. I have her conducting an investigation with Ray to find out what he knows."

Olivia nodded. "This is all so . . . strange."

Anna reached across the table, putting her hand on Olivia's. "It will be fine. I think you have an appointment this evening with the Cullinan police, right?"

"Yes," Olivia said. Kirk had told her about it right before the Savage Seven had arrived. She looked at the doorway, wishing he'd appear. She knew that Anna was highly skilled, but it was Kirk who made her feel safe.

"Do you think they need us?" Olivia asked.

"No. But if you'd feel better hearing their discussions, we can go in there," Anna said.

"Will we be disturbing them?"

"No. Let's go."

She followed Anna down the hall to the living room command center. The men were talking quietly but stopped when they entered.

"Sorry to intrude, but we wanted to know what was going on," Anna said.

"Just going over the details for tonight. Mann suggested we put listening devices in Lambert's office so we can monitor his activities. See if we can catch him doing or saying something illegal," Savage said.

"Is that okay for us to do?" Olivia asked.

"Once we know what he's doing, we'll alert the authorities and bring them with us to make an arrest," Kirk said.

Olivia nodded. She trusted Kirk. "What can I do to help?"

"We have a copy of the plans for the Onyx Mines office building . . . can you show us which office is Lambert's?" Savage asked.

She went over to the table where the plans were laid out. The men all moved out of her way. She looked at the schematic but couldn't identify Lambert's office on the plans.

"You have an old copy. They just did a big renovation."

"Great. This is the most up-to-date one I found on file," Laz said.

"Do you know where his office is?" Savage asked.

"Yes. It's on the top floor."

"That's all we need. You can go with us," Savage said.

"She'll stay in the command vehicle and I'll protect her," Kirk said.

"Agreed."

Burati and Barack entered the Onyx Mine offices just before midnight. They'd already spent two hours installing digital cameras in all of the mine shafts on the property. Burati had orders about the kind of information that Phillip wanted them to gather. He left his cousin going through the files while he placed the bugs in the phone and under the desk.

"Are you sure about this?" Barack asked.

"Sure about what? This is our job. Don't ask questions, just work."

"I don't understand how you can still work for the man who killed Thomas."

Burati ignored his cousin and just kept working. He had never been one of those men to explain himself to others. He made his decisions and he lived by them. That was all there was to it.

He placed the last bug and climbed up on the credenza in

the corner of the office to place a digital camera lens that was smaller than a straight pin. He wedged the camera under the ceiling tile. The camera connected wirelessly to a receiver unit that he was going to set up down the hallway in a maintenance closet.

"I'll be back," he said to Barack.

He got the recorder set up in the closet and tested it, watching as Barack went in and out of the office checking files and making copies.

Satisfied with the work he'd done, he went back down the hall and joined his cousin.

Barack was silent as they continued to work. "I do this for Thomas. I do this so that the man who killed him will spend a long time in jail."

Barack nodded and they both worked in silence, finishing their tasks as quickly as possible. Burati called Phillip before they left the compound.

"Did you get everything set up like I asked?" Phillip asked.

"Indeed I did."

"Good. Now we will be able to track his every move. Olivia's parents have hired an investigator to help find her. The company is Liberty Investigations."

"Mr. Ray had me look into a friend of Olivia's who works for them—Anna Sterling."

"Well, Charity Keone-Williams will be the woman who is conducting the investigation."

"Should I be helpful?" Burati asked. He wanted to do whatever he could to help end this mess.

"Only if Lambert isn't around. I don't want to risk anything happening to the Pontufs."

Olivia didn't know what to do about Kirk. She knew he was a dangerous man—she had seen that with her own eyes—but she realized that didn't matter. It scared her each time he revealed something new about himself, because he was everything she should have been afraid of, yet he didn't scare her.

They were both dressed in black from head to toe and were outfitted with earpiece wireless communicators in their ears. They were with the Savage Seven team and a Cullinan police detective named Sandoval who was conducting the murder investigation.

"This is where I saw him shoot the other man. It was in the distance, but I could clearly see Ray's gun and the other man fall."

"Good. I'll send my men out to scout the location in the morning," Sandoval said.

Twenty minutes later they were seated in a Range Rover in the downtown area of Cullinan watching the Savage Seven team via a video monitor that was mounted on Savage's glasses.

Olivia was sitting as quietly as she could, knowing that they didn't need any extra chatter on the line, but she was nervous and wanted to talk.

Since it was nighttime and dark the images were grainy infrared ones. Anna, Savage, Hamm, and Wenz were all spread out around the main offices of the Onyx Diamond Group as well. Laz and Jacob were both hanging back.

Jacob was the command central for this midnight operation and Laz was the transportation guy. It was a bit breezy and Olivia worried that she should have stayed at the safe house.

"You okay?" Kirk asked.

"Yes, fine. A little nervous."

"Don't worry, Olivia," Anna said via the earpiece. "Mann won't let anything happen to you."

"I know," Olivia said. She watched Kirk as they sat in the

dark and waited. He was steady, rock steady, with his weapon in position. He was silent when he moved and she realized he was the best at what he did.

She'd be silly to worry when he was by her side, because he'd die to protect her. She leaned over, wanting to kiss him, but stopped.

Her reactions to him were getting out of control. She was falling for this guy. He was supersexy, so that didn't really surprise her, but it did worry her. She'd never felt a sexual attraction anything near this intense.

"One in place," Wenz said.

"Two in place," Hamm said.

"Three in place," Anna said.

"Four in place," Savage said.

"Five and Six in place."

"We are entering the building," Savage said.

"It's weird to hear everyone but not see them," Olivia said. She didn't think she'd ever adjust to doing stuff like this, but it was kind of fun. And it was giving her some ideas for the next Krissie Carmichael book. She was definitely going to use the codes and words she'd learned from the Savage Seven.

"You get used to it," Kirk said.

"Follow me," Savage said, leading the team into the building. "We're going silent now."

She watched as they worked their way through the deserted office building toward the executive level by way of the fire escapes.

She was the only member of the team without a weapon tonight. But she hadn't wanted one. She didn't know how to handle a weapon and knew that she'd be more of a liability to herself if she had one.

"You are going the wrong way," she said. "Savage?"

"Affirmative."

"Sorry for talking, but I didn't want us to waste any time."

"It's okay. Which way?"

"Left."

The team entered the office and startled two men already there. Olivia gasped as she recognized Burati and Barack.

"Those are the men who tried to kidnap me."

"What is he doing there?" Olivia asked.

"Savage will find out."

Kirk had a sick feeling in his gut as he watched the team escape down the fire exit. He'd seen the fight on screen of the team and Burati and Barack. Savage was bringing both men back for questioning.

He wanted to hurt Burati and the other guard for laying their hands on Olivia at the airport.

"Where are the men in the car?" Savage asked.

Kirk checked the other monitor, keeping an eye on the guards at the mine.

"Sitting in the car. Did the guard alert them?"

"I have no idea," Savage said. "He didn't say anything, but they may have a silent signal."

"Is Burati still unconscious?" Kirk asked.

"Affirmative. Did Hamm get the other guard?"

"Yes. They went out the back, but you can't leave the fire escape until the men in the BMW are gone," Kirk said. "I can send Laz in with the retrieval vehicle to distract them."

Everyone stood still while they waited for Savage's decision. He was the leader of the team and they all followed him. It had been odd having Savage back on the team. He'd been working in the office in London since his wedding to Anna, and having him back had made Kirk realize how much he'd missed having his friend in the field.

"No. I'll provide the distraction. Laz, have the transport ready to roll as soon as the team gets to you," Savage said.

"Where will you be?" Anna asked.

"Doing my job, babe," Savage replied.

"Jack Savage . . . you better make it back home to me," she said.

"I will. I've got too much to live for," he said.

Kirk realized he felt the same way about Olivia. Maybe not as intense as what Savage felt for Anna, but he knew he didn't want to lose the woman he'd found. Didn't want to take any stupid risks so he wouldn't make it back to her. "Wenz, you go with Savage," Kirk said.

"Wait a minute—I'm in charge," Savage said.

"You need backup. Unless you want me to go high and just take both men out?"

"No," Olivia said.

He glanced over at her. She was shaking and pale but very determined. "Let's get everyone out of here."

"I agree," Anna said.

"The men are moving toward the entrance. I'll give you a signal when you are good to go," Jacob said.

They waited tensely for less than sixty seconds and then Van said to move.

The three of them in the emergency staircase moved quickly out of the door. Van was slowed a little by carrying the weight of Burati, but he kept moving. He couldn't watch their back, which made him nervous, but less than a minute later, Hamm joined them with the other guard over his shoulder.

"Savage is to the left," Hamm said.

They moved in an open formation toward the vehicles where Laz and Van waited. Kirk wished he was there in the thick of the action. But Olivia only felt safe with him and protecting her came first.

"I'm glad they are out of the building."

Kirk didn't tell her that they weren't in the clear yet, that a sniper's bullet could easily kill one of them from this distance.

He kept his eyes peeled and was hypervigilant. This job was personal to him. For the first time the mission wasn't just about a paycheck but about a person.

And he'd promised Olivia he'd keep her alive, so he wasn't going to let anything happen to her.

Hamm's silhouette was clearly visible against the night sky and Kirk prayed that the men who'd entered the building stayed there. He didn't want a firefight tonight. He wanted an easy end to this FUBAR mess that the night had become.

Wenz went next and then only Savage remained.

"I've got your back," Kirk said.

"You're one of the few guys I trust there," Savage said.

"Don't I know it? Go on. I'm getting itchy."

"Me, too. Something feels wrong about this entire thing."

"You two can discuss it later," Van said in their earpieces. "Move ass."

Savage went up the incline in a smooth and easy run. The rest of the team was already moving forward toward the two vehicles they'd brought with them.

The large army-style vehicles were hidden in the brush far from the road.

"Haul ass," Van said. "They know we are still on the property and are heading toward your location."

Everyone started to move. "I've got it," Wenz said, stopping to cover them as they all retreated.

"I'll be back as soon as I dump this guy," Van said.

"No, you won't. Keep moving," Wenz said. "We need to get out of here."

Kirk didn't agree. He wanted to lay some ground fire and let Lambert know he wasn't messing with an amateur. Make damned sure that Lambert realized he was going to have go through hell to get to Olivia and capture her again.

And Kirk realized that he wasn't taking any more chances

with her safety. From now on Savage and the rest of the Savage Seven were going to have to realize that he was protecting Olivia first and foremost.

They were all in the vehicle and he breathed a sigh of relief as he climbed into the driver's seat. "Get your seat belt on. We are heading home."

He was going to have answers from Burati either the hard way or the easy way.

Chapter Sixteen

Burati had been interrogated before. In fact, this wasn't the first time he'd been taken by men who weren't cops. But he was South African and had grown up during apartheid, so he didn't scare easily. Barack, on the other hand, looked nervous and scared.

When the man who'd taken Olivia from him at the airport entered, Burati didn't even try to pretend he didn't know what the man wanted. "You are Kirk, right? Who do you work for?"

"I'll ask the questions," the man said.

"I'm Leon Burati and I work for Phillip Michaels at the Diamond Consortium."

"I will check this out and come right back."

"Very well. My cousin was simply helping me out tonight. He has no information," Burati said.

"If this is true, he will be let go."

Kirk left and Burati turned to his cousin. "Don't worry—you'll be out of here soon."

"What about you?"

"I am more involved in everything that is happening here. So I won't be going home for a while."

Burati relaxed as best he could with his hands tied behind his back to a chair. His head ached. He hadn't felt this bad since he'd been a boy. He'd grown up in poverty and violence was a part of everyday life. It seemed no matter how much he tried, violence was the one thing he couldn't escape. His mother used to say that once a boy took a step down the path of violence the man he became was doomed to always walk it.

That woman had always been right.

The door opened twenty minutes later and Kirk came back in with another man. "Your story checks out. One of our men will take your cousin back to his vehicle or wherever he wants to go."

Kirk untied both men and Barack hesitated. "Do you need me?"

"No, I'll be fine," Burati said.

Barack left and Burati was alone with Kirk.

"Phillip will be calling you in a few minutes to authorize you to talk to us. In the meantime, can I get you something to drink?"

"Water would be nice," Burati said.

His mobile phone rang just as Kirk returned with the water. "Burati here."

"It's Phillip. I've talked to Kirk Mann. He has Olivia and is working in conjunction with her friend Anna. Please share whatever information you deem necessary and call me back after you leave there."

"I will, sir. The camera and bugs are in place."

"Thanks, Burati. I am already getting signals from both."

"Good. Maybe we are on our way to finally seeing justice served."

"I think we are," Phillip said.

Burati hung up his phone and turned to look at Kirk. "What questions do you have for me?"

"What were you doing at Onyx tonight?"

"Installing some listening and digital recording devices. The consortium needs hard proof that Lambert is stealing from them. They had a man on the inside, but he was murdered."

"Olivia witnessed it."

To think if he'd followed her when she'd gone to the mines that day he would have seen his own brother killed. Maybe he could have done something to save Thomas. But he'd never know.

"The man who was killed was my brother."

"Then you have a personal reason for going after Lambert."

"Yes, I do. But I'm in no hurry. Justice waits until the man is ready."

"Indeed it does," Kirk said.

The men discussed what each of them wanted and Burati found that Kirk was a man he could respect. He realized that Olivia was in a safe place as long as Kirk was watching over her. He apologized for the knife wound he'd inflicted on Kirk and they exchanged mobile numbers to keep each other apprised of any situations that developed.

Burati was blindfolded and taken back to his vehicle. Phillip called him one more time to say that they had enough evidence with what the Savage Seven had gathered to go to the prosecutor and have Ray Lambert arrested. That news made him very happy.

Olivia didn't stay with the group when they arrived back at the safe house. She went straight upstairs to her room. She closed the door and sank down on the floor. Pulling her knees up to her chest, she breathed deeply and tried to convince herself that she was safe now. She'd known that Kirk wouldn't let anything happen to her, but watching things tonight . . . she hadn't felt safe.

But she knew it wasn't physical safety that she had lost. It was that inner security that most people carried around inside them. Tonight had reinforced what she'd started to realize the other day when Ray had tried to shoot her and then her own bodyguard had tried to kidnap her: she had no safe place any more. The world had turned into someplace she no longer could identify. She knew that Anna and the others needed her to read over the papers they'd gotten from Ray's office, and she was determined not to let them down. But right now she was still shaking inside and she needed to be here.

She didn't want to think where Kirk might be. She had seen how angry he was when Burati had hit her at the airport and she was very afraid that he'd do something violent in retalia-tion. And she knew now that he was the kind of man who'd exact that kind of justice . . . vigilante justice, she thought. He didn't need a judge and jury to tell him if someone was guilty or not. He made that decision on his own.

There was a knock on her door.

"Who is it?"

"Kirk."

He was exactly who she wanted to see, and yet she was afraid to see him right now because she was really leaning on him. She didn't say anything, just stayed where she was crouched on the floor like a child. She hadn't hidden like this since . . . never. She'd never felt this vulnerable before. And it was affecting her.

"You okay?" he asked.

"Yes. Do you want to come in?"

"Yes," he said.

He pushed open the door and entered. She stared at his boots and his pant legs.

He stooped down in front of her. "Are you okay?"

She nodded. "Just scared."

"You should have a shower. It'll help you relax."

She tried to stand up, but her ankle shifted under her and she swayed a little, almost falling over. He caught her up in his arms. She put her arms around his shoulders and rested her face against his neck. Her cheek felt the warmth of his skin and she realized that she'd never felt like this before, like her body wasn't her own.

"I should have kept you here."

"They needed me. Savage was going the wrong way. I needed to be useful and not sit here and wait."

"You aren't suited to that kind of op. From now on you stay here."

"I . . . okay."

"Shower now," Kirk said, stepping back.

"I don't have anything to change in to," she said.

"I asked Laz to get you something to sleep in while he was out gathering supplies for us today."

"You did?"

"Yes," Kirk said. "Get in the shower and I'll leave it on the sink for you."

He disappeared into the bedroom and she turned to look at herself in the mirror. Her eyes were huge in her face and she hardly recognized herself.

She started to cry looking at it and didn't hear Kirk when he reentered the bathroom. "Baby, don't cry."

She nodded and took a deep breath.

But deep inside she wasn't sure she'd ever be fine again. Every day brought another new thing for her to process and get over. Each day, that process was just a little bit harder.

"I'm sorry for crying."

He thumbed the tears off her face and rubbed his fingers together. "Don't be."

"Stay with me," she said. Going up on tiptoe, she kissed him.

His lips were still under hers for a second and then he kissed her back. "If I stay I'm going to make love to you."

"Good."

He reached around her and adjusted the water temperature and then turned the shower on. He came back to her and carefully undressed her and then took off his own clothes. It was then she saw that he'd been hurt at some point. He had a wound on his left side that was bleeding through the bandage he'd put on it.

"What happened to you?" she asked. She reached out to touch the bandage. How had she missed him getting hurt? She hated that he was already so scarred. Not because the marks marred his body but because of the pain he had to have endured to get them.

"It's from another mission. I tore it when I was working out with Laz earlier," Kirk said. His eyes were very chilling and cold when he looked at her.

He lifted her up and stepped into the shower with her in his arms. He let the spray hit him first and slowly set her on her feet.

She knew she needed to wash up and get clean, but right at that moment she just needed his arms around her. She leaned her uninjured cheek against his thickly muscled chest and wrapped her arms around his lean waist.

Kirk put his arms around her and held her just as tightly as she held him. Olivia wanted to pretend that this was a normal part of building a relationship, but she wasn't too sure about that. There was nothing regular about her life now. She was going to just live in the moment with Kirk. She needed him. Needed him like this and that's all that she knew.

She lifted her head and kissed him right over his heart, then rested her cheek over his left pectoral. She heard the solid beating of his heart under her ear and it made her feel infinitely better.

Kirk was the man she'd been searching for her entire life, but she'd never realized it until now. She would have never thought to look for a man like him, but he was exactly what she needed.

They got out of the shower and Kirk tenderly dried her off. It was all she could do to keep from breaking down and sobbing out loud. She realized she didn't want him to see that utterly weak side of her.

He pulled a plain brown bag across the vanity and opened it up, pulling at an exquisite negligee. It was black lace with a pretty pattern on it and when he drew it over her head and down her body she shivered a little.

No man had ever given her something like this before. This was a garment meant for a lover. And she realized that to Kirk she was this kind of woman.

"What do you see in me?" she asked softly as he turned to towel dry. She knew she wasn't much in the looks department. She could clean up good for a party and she knew how to socialize, but those were hardly skills that mattered to a man like Kirk. What drew him to her?

Or was she simply someone to scratch an itch?

"What did you say?" he asked.

She couldn't say it again. She took a deep breath, realizing she could mumble something else and never have this conversation. "I'm tired and I'm scared and I just want this all to end."

The words were more a reminder for her of how crazy her life had become. No matter how real it felt to be in his arms, this was still about nothing more than sex. She almost hoped he'd get angry and leave. Then she could just crawl into bed and pull the covers over her head and never leave.

He started tickling her. His fingers moved over her until she laughed without meaning to until she started crying. She hoped she could pretend that they were tears of mirth, but then her breath caught on a ragged sigh. Tears started rolling down her face and she started crying, really crying.

She turned away from him and buried her face in one of her hands. She couldn't stop the tears and she had no idea where they'd come from. Oh, damn, she wasn't doing this. She had to get it together.

He put one hand on her shoulder and tried to draw her back into his arms, but she fought him. She didn't want to be in his arms again, didn't want to feel that sense of rightness and that feeling that she never wanted to move again.

He lifted her into his arms and carried her into the bedroom. He threw back the covers on the bed with one hand and then set her down in the middle of the bed. He settled over her. He lowered his head, slowly licking at the tracks of her tears down her face. She closed her eyes, but that only intensified the feeling of Kirk. His chest against her breasts, his groin against hers, his legs twined with hers.

"Open your eyes, baby," he said.

And she wasn't going to open her eyes. Not now when she felt so raw and stripped bare of everything. How come he was the man who'd made her feel like this?

She opened her eyes and met his serious grayeyed gaze. He had that ability to completely focus on one thing, as she'd seen tonight, and right now he was bringing that concentration to her.

She looked up at him and tried to find the words to tell him that she no longer felt like Olivia Pontuf but now felt like a hollowed-out shell of that woman, who had no idea how she was going to survive.

And survival was the important lesson she'd carried with her from tonight.

Of course, she could trust Kirk. He was a solid man. *A good man.* "You're a good man, Kirk. And you know who you are, but I'm floundering here. I'm scared and a liability."

He lowered his mouth over hers, kissed her with so much tenderness that she wrenched her head to the side, breaking the kiss. She didn't want a tender lover. She didn't want Kirk to touch her with caring in his eyes. She didn't want him to make love to her. She'd have sex with him, so she could forget her fear.

"I'm a complete coward. I was so scared the entire time. I wanted to just start screaming and never stop."

"But you didn't."

How did he see that? "I don't feel like that right now."

"You are tired."

"I'm used up inside," she said quietly, being as honest as she could be with him.

He rolled to his side, pulling her into his arms, cradling her. *Cherishing her.* She didn't know where the thought came from, but when he pulled her into his arms she always felt cherished in a way that Ray had never made her feel. In fact, no man had ever made her feel like this before. Only Kirk.

She heard the steady beat of his heart under her ear. It soothed the scared part of her. His arms were muscled and strong and his shoulders wide enough to carry any burden.

She pushed against his chest, trying to get up, but he held her securely in his arms. "I'm sorry for breaking down like that. Don't you have to go back downstairs?"

"No, not now. I only have to take care of you," he said.

She tried not to let those words matter, but they did, and that scared her more than facing down Burati with a gun. Because she realized she was starting to fall in love with Kirk Mann. And that was at once the most wonderful feeling in the world and also a little bit scary, because she had no idea how to be in love.

*   *   *

"Really?"

He nodded. He wasn't like the kind of men she was used to and he had no words to tell her how he really felt. But he could show her. She looked so pretty in the negligee he'd asked Laz to pick up in Johannesburg.

He knew she was used to the finer things and this gown was more suited to her than his T-shirt.

He was going to use the physical bond between them to bind her to him tonight because he wanted her.

"You are sexy," she said.

"Am I?"

She laughed, but the mirth didn't reach her eyes. He noticed there were still tears in the corner of her eye and he carefully wiped them away. "You have a very nice body."

"I have to keep in shape. Have to stay honed," he said. Realizing that kind of talk wasn't going to relax her. "I like to work out."

"Why? I hate any exercise except for running. Running always makes me feel free."

That was an interesting tidbit. She revealed pieces of herself in small increments and he could do nothing other than gather them up and tuck them away. Add the pieces together and try to make them fit until he had her figured out.

"Tell me about this scar," she said, finding one of his more wicked knife scars. It started above his abdomen and continued to his hip and went down the back of his left butt cheek and thigh.

She lifted one eyebrow at him. Her breasts brushed his side as she leaned up over him. He reached down and caught her nipple between his fingers. He loved the velvet texture of her nipple.

He cupped her breast fully in his palm, continuing to stroke

her finger across her nipple. She shifted around a little, pushing her breast more fully into his grasp.

She stroked her hands over his chest. Each pass she came
closer and closer to his cock but never touched him.

"A toughie like you must have ways of making people
talk," she said. "What can I do to get you to open up to me?"

He shrugged. He knew the image he presented to the
world was one big badass. He *was* that man, but with Olivia he
couldn't be.

"Please tell me about this scar."

"I can't tell you too many details. But we were on a mission
to take out the leader of a terrorist cell."

"Were you undercover?"

He nodded. "I'm good at blending in."

"So you were there surrounded by the enemy. Then what
happened?"

"I wasn't alone," he said. "Armand was with me."

"He's your friend who died, right?" she asked. She was
holding on to his bicep and stroking him as he talked. He
doubted she was even aware of it, but he liked it.

"Yes. Armand and I were disguised as militants who'd come
from another faction to join this terror cell. Someone caught
wind that we weren't who we said we were, and we were
brought to the leader for questioning."

"Oh, Kirk. How many times have you been in a life-and-
death situation and survived?"

He shrugged. More than he wanted to count.

She rubbed her other hand over his scar. "What happened
next?"

"They disarmed us and took a try at getting us to talk," he
said remembering the bloody mess they'd left behind. They'd
been working for the U.S. government at that time and they
had wanted to question the terror cell leader to try to get

closer to bin Laden, but he and Armand hadn't been able to take anyone alive.

They'd both been close to death's door by the time they'd gotten out of the camp. They'd left nothing behind but a burning a mess. They had taken a few new scars with them.

She kept caressing his hip as he told his tale. He liked the way it felt, almost like caring. That was what he really wanted with her. He wanted to wrap himself around her and make her forget that she thought she was used up inside.

"You are so strong," she said.

He started laughing, remembering that Armand had carried him out of the camp.

"What are you laughing at?" she asked.

"Well, I'm not the supermacho badass you might think I am," he said.

"I think you are," she said as she tangled her fingers in the hair right above his groin.

"Heroic," she said, skimming her finger along the side of his thigh. He spread his legs wider to accommodate her, loving the feel of her hands on his skin.

He shrugged. "I'm not a hero. I'm just a guy doing his job."

"No, you're not. You're so much more than that. You're my hero, and I doubt you will ever realize how much you mean to me."

He hoped he could live up to her words. He needed to be the man she saw him as, because he'd never had anyone believe in him before. Never had a woman look at him the way that she did.

She kept touching him and it was having a pronounced effect on him. She smiled up at him when his erection stirred, growing harder.

"Are you done talking?" she asked him.

There was no maybe about it. He skimmed his hand down her curvy figure. She fondled his erection, resting her head on his lower stomach. He felt each exhalation of her breath against his cock.

He put his hand on her head, wrapping his fingers through her hair and rubbing the back of her head. She shifted around until she was lying between his spread legs, looking up at him.

Having her between his legs, his hand on her head, he drew her toward his erection. She smiled up at him and licked the tip of him. His hips jerked up in reaction.

Stroking his length while she sucked on the tip of his penis, she had him in the palm of her hand. She took him into her mouth and he thought he'd die from the sweet ecstasy of her.

He drew her up his body before he spilled himself in her mouth. He reached for a condom with one hand and donned it quickly. He tested her and found her body warm, wet, and ready for him.

She straddled him and he entered in her in one smooth motion. She rode him hard, her breasts bouncing with each movement, and they both climbed quickly toward their climax, shuddering together and crying each other's names. Then she collapsed against his chest and he held her tightly, knowing he wasn't letting her go.

Kirk had never had sex like this before. Olivia simply rocked his world and his soul and made him feel like he couldn't survive without her.

And he was a survivor, he'd always been. But that didn't really rattle him too much. He'd been good at adapting to situations and figuring out how to keep himself alive.

What bothered him was the fact that Olivia was a part of him now. He wasn't a loner anymore. She might not even realize that she'd changed him, but she had.

He rolled them both to their sides and tucked her up close to him. She put her head on his chest right over his heart and he bent down to kiss the top of her head.

As he held her next to him he made a vow to always be

there for her and to protect her. This was beyond whatever favor Savage had wanted the team to do for an old friend of Anna's. This was his vow to his woman.

Without question, Olivia Pontuf had become more than a job to him.

Chapter Seventeen

Olivia woke in the middle of the night, startled for a minute at the feel of a man's arm around her. *Kirk*. His heat surrounded her completely. She skimmed her fingers over his arm down to his wrist, sliding her fingers through his until they were joined.

What was she going to do? Nothing had been settled and she knew that they both probably were needed downstairs to analyze the files that they had gotten out of Ray's office tonight. But right now she just wanted to stay right here.

He'd made love to her and then they'd drifted off to sleep. Her body ached in places she hadn't known it could. The room smelled of sex and the scent of Kirk. There was no clock in the room that she could see, but the room was lightening as the sun began to rise. She didn't want the night to end, but she knew she couldn't hide from the new day. She had to face everything that was going on around her.

She had made her decision. She'd ask Kirk to teach her some self-defense moves so she didn't feel so out of her element the next time she was confronted with someone like Burati. Kirk's hand tightened under hers. His cock hardened against her butt and he slid his hand up her body to cup her breast. She glanced over her shoulder at him.

She knew he saw the questions and indecision on her face, but when he would have spoken, she turned in his arms and took his mouth with hers, kissed him so that the words he would speak couldn't be heard.

She closed her eyes and held on to his shoulders and pretended that this was all a pretty dream because she needed this moment to be real. She needed the emotions he elicited in her to be true. He sucked her tongue into his mouth and nibbled on it. She liked the way he tasted first thing in the morning.

He fondled her breasts, rubbing his palms over her nipples until they were hard and aching for his mouth. She shifted her leg up over his hip, felt the roughness of his scar against her inner thigh. Remembered the craziness of his bold actions. Remembered that at the end of the day Kirk was a hero, though he'd never call himself one.

His erection rubbed against her. She rocked against it, rubbing her wetness up and down his cock. He lifted his head for a second to smile down at her. There was something in that smile that she didn't want to acknowledge. A real tenderness and caring that she wasn't sure she was ready to recognize between them.

She leaned over him, reaching for the condoms on the nightstand. He bent and caught her nipple between his lips, suckling her sweetly, strongly, drawing hard on her nipple until she moaned his name. Her hands holding his head, the condom falling forgotten in the sheets.

She rubbed her center against his hard-on, trying to get closer to him. Trying to assuage an ache that she was only now realizing was so much more than physical.

He switched to her other breast, then slid down her body.

His fingers caressed her between her legs. His finger circled her opening before dipping into her and taking her own moisture and using it to lubricate his fingers as he caressed her clitoris. She squirmed under his touch, reaching for his cock, drawing him closer to her.

She shifted around on the bed so that he was poised at the entrance of her body. He entered her, just the tip, then pulled back.

"Condom?"

Where had she dropped it? She rolled over to look for it. His hands massaged her back all the way down to her buttocks, then she felt the searing heat of his mouth on her. The warm wet kisses that lingered over each inch of her skin. He nibbled on the cheeks of her backside and then tongued the crease between them. No one had ever touched her there, and she wasn't sure where it would lead now.

She squirmed, needing more from him. She felt his hand on her at her entrance, dipping into her center and then tracing a teasing pattern over her backside. She shifted away from his probing fingers and found the condom, trying to turn over to hand it to him.

"Stay like this," he said. She heard him rip open the condom and turned in time to see him donning it. She tried to roll onto her back again. It might be better if she couldn't see his face. If somehow she could force him back into the sex-toy category. As if he'd ever been there.

But he put his hand in the center of her back and held her still. Then he slid down next to her on the bed and drew her back in his arms. He pulled her top leg back over her hips so that she was open to him.

She felt his hand on her mound, his palm between her legs, stretching her open to accommodate him. Then the tip of his cock was nestled at her opening. He rocked against her, teasing her with just that small penetration.

But she needed more. She needed him. Needed him deep inside her so that she could not think about the impact this night was going to have on her. She was desperate to have him inside her.

She reached between their open legs, circled her hand around the base of his cock, and squeezed lightly putting enough pressure on him that he jerked against her, then slid further into her body. He rested his thumb against her clit and rubbed it up and down while he kept up the leisurely thrusting in and out of her.

His other hand came up to her breast, pinching her nipples lightly at first but then harder as his thrusts increased and the pressure grew between them.

She reached lower, scoring his sac with her fingernails. She felt his teeth against her shoulder, a small bite followed by a soothing kiss and his tongue against her neck.

He thrust harder against her, and she felt everything inside her building toward her orgasm. She came fast and hard and heard him shout her name in her ear. She shook with the physical sensations rushing through her but also the emotional upheaval.

The fact was that no matter how hard she tried to make this feel normal it never was going to be. Kirk wasn't like the other men she'd had in her life. And she thanked God for it as he held her tenderly in his arms. He was all man and he made her want to be all woman, with all of a woman's strengths.

He held her tenderly as he continued thrusting into her, riding out his climax and extending hers until another wave rose.

She gripped his thigh, her nails digging into his leg. Before he turned her in his arms and kissed with long drugging kisses that made it easy for her to drift back to sleep with his arms around her, made it easy to forget that she wasn't going to get used to his arms around her. This was for one night. As she drifted off, she snuggled closer to him.

She curled herself around him and wrapped his strength around her. She pretended that he was hers forever and not just until she was safe again. That thought helped her drift off in peaceful slumber and made sure that she didn't have night-mares.

Kirk got out of bed, careful not to wake Olivia. He watched her sleeping, admired the lacy negligee draped over her body. He found his pants and his weapon and walked out of the bedroom. Downstairs he found Laz on guard duty.

"Where is everyone?"

"Savage and Hamm are still with Burati—he called them last night and asked to work with us to set a trap for Lambert. Wenz and Van are watching the Onyx Mine to make sure that we know when Lambert makes a move. Both men are good at what they do and at keeping quiet."

"So you haven't found anything yet?"

"Not really. Anna's been working on the files we got, but I think she needs to ask Olivia a few questions."

"She's still sleeping," Kirk said.

"You're mighty protective of that woman . . ."

"Don't, Laz."

Laz looked up at him. "I'm not saying a word."

But Laz didn't have to. Kirk understood that a woman like Olivia could mess a man up, mess up his thinking, and a guy who didn't think could end up dead. "I'm still focused on the job."

"I'd never think you weren't."

"Is there anything in the kitchen for breakfast?" Kirk asked Laz, needing to get away from his teammate and back to his woman. Some time during the night he'd realized that she was his.

"There's some fresh fruit in the fridge and some rolls. That's it."

"Thanks," Kirk said. He went in the kitchen and made a tray of food for Olivia and himself, then carried it back upstairs.

He let himself into the bedroom, locking the door behind him. He put the tray on the nightstand and then took off his jeans. He crawled back into the bed with her and kissed her awake.

"Morning," he said.

She stretched and smiled up at him sleepily. He knew that this moment might be the last quiet one they had together.

"Good morning."

"Want some breakfast?"

"Yes, please."

He handed her a mug of coffee and then propped the pillows up behind her so they could both lean back against them. He moved her around until she was seated between his legs with her back resting against his chest.

He put her coffee mug back on the tray and brought over the bowl of chilled strawberries.

He held the bowl away from her when she reached for the container. "Lean back against me. I want to feed you."

"What, no please?"

"Please."

He decided he wanted to see and shifted them both so that he lay on his back and drew her down next to him. He leaned on his elbow so that he looked down at her. He opened the container and took out one of the strawberries. He rubbed it against her lips until she opened them, then inserted just the tip of the berry between her teeth. She took a bite. Juice dripped down her chin.

He caught it with his tongue, then drew her lower lip between his teeth and suckled on it. She opened her mouth on a sigh. "This feels sinful to me."

"Me, too. I've never done this before," he said.

"Had breakfast in bed?"

"Yup. I'm usually an eating a bowl of cereal over the sink kind of guy," he said.

"I usually skip breakfast. No man's ever brought me breakfast in bed before."

He was glad he'd been the first to do it. He had done it . . . because he wanted her to start feeling normal. Knew she needed to stop being so afraid if she was going to adjust to getting back to her real life.

"Take the top of your negligee down."

She reached up and slipped the straps down her arms. The bodice of the nightgown loosened, but the fabric still covered her breasts. He brushed the straps aside and ran the juicy berry along her collarbone, bending to trace the trail left by the juice with his tongue.

She reached between them and caressed his chest. He liked her hands on his skin, loved the way she always touched him despite his scarred body. "You lie back."

He did as she asked, and she leaned over him, the fabric of her negligee falling down to reveal the curves of her pretty breasts. He rubbed the berry he still had in his hand over her nipples, then leaned up to lick the juice off her. She moaned his name and arched her back. He wrapped one arm around her and continued to lick and suckle her breasts.

She shifted around on his lap until she straddled him. He lifted his head when she tugged on his hair. She put a ripe berry between his teeth and he bit down on it. Juice slipped from the edge of his mouth into hers. Her tongue tangled with his. The kiss was sweet and hot.

She pushed on his shoulders, urging him onto his back. She used the berry in her hand to trace circles on his chest, around his nipples and then down the line of hair that disappeared under the waistband of his pants. She leaned down, rubbing her breasts against him, and then licked the juice off him.

He pulled the hem of her nightgown up her legs until it was bunched at her waist.

"Lay on top of me," he said.

She lowered herself on top of him, but he stopped her. "On your back."

"What?"

"Trust me. You'll like this."

He wanted to make love to her again but didn't want to look in her eyes. He shifted her until she was reclined on top of him. She nestled her head on his shoulder. He brought his hands up to cup her breasts and teased them.

He reached between her legs. She was already damp. He loved how hot she got for him. He dipped one finger into her and she shivered against him.

His erection was trapped between their bodies and he reached down with his other hand to free himself. He found the condom he'd left on the nightstand earlier and sheathed himself with it.

Olivia's wrist came over his and shifted her legs on top of his. He slipped the head of his cock into her body. He couldn't get deep penetration this way, but it still felt good.

Olivia shifted on top of him. One of her legs fell outside his. She put her right palm against the base of his shaft as she shifted up and then back down. He felt the metal of her rings against his hot skin. She moved slowly, building tension between them. He fondled her breast with one hand.

They rocked together until the tension built and then he felt her shuddering around him. He shifted her off his body, pulling his erection out of her. Settling himself over her, he thrust deep, driving into her three times before his own climax rocked through his body. He cradled her close in his arms, knowing all he could do was keep her safe and get rid of Lambert. Then it would be time to move on once again.

*   *   *

Olivia felt raw from all the lovemaking with Kirk. He made her feel more alive or maybe it was that she was simply taking the time to enjoy being alive after having come so close to dying.

She didn't really want to think about what could have been tonight. Kirk was way too real and too here for her to be thinking of another man. They'd both had a shower and gotten dressed and she knew it was time to head downstairs and help Anna with her search through Ray's files. But she needed one more moment with Kirk.

"Hold me," she said.

He put his gun in his shoulder holster and came over, drawing her into his arms. Standing in the middle of her bedroom, she rested her head on his shoulder and felt the strength implicit in the way he held her. She felt a kind of bond that went deeper than sex, which scared the hell out of her.

She could understand an attachment to him that came from his making her feel safe. He had one hand in her hair, his fingers massaging the back of her neck and the other hand at her waist. She tipped her head back, met his warm gray gaze, and realized that she wasn't going to hide anymore. Not from herself, him, or the blatant sexuality that he brought effortlessly to the surface.

"Come to bed with me, Kirk. Make love to me one more time before we go out there and face the world. I want to take your scent and some of your strength with me today."

He didn't say a word as she led him back to bed. She had made the bed and the neat-looking room was a statement of her old life, she thought. Everything looked safe and secure and not a thing was. That had been a lie and this fierce-looking man had made her realize the truth.

She'd let herself grow dead inside and she wanted desperately to feel alive again. To feel alive the way she did in Kirk's arms. The way she had only when his arms were wrapped around her.

"This place feels like it shouldn't feel like home," she said. "It's nothing like my bedroom. Yet it does. What's your place like?"

She had no idea what Kirk's home would look like.

"Umm, it's kind of empty. I have an apartment where I crash between jobs. It's nothing special," he said, sitting on the edge of her bed and drawing her closer to him between his spread thighs.

He hugged her tight and she realized for the first time that he had secrets of his own. She'd been so busy protecting hers that she felt a little silly just now realizing that there was a reason why Kirk was the man he was today.

He rolled onto his back, pulling her down on top of him. She slid her hands under his shirt against his skin. He urged her head back and kissed her like they had all day. Like he'd be happy to hold her and just kiss forever.

It was a sweet moment here in the bedroom and she let her mind drift away as a fire started to build inside her. She moved restlessly against him as he licked a path from her chin down the side of her neck.

He traced the neckline of her shirt with his fingertip as he kissed her there. She tunneled her fingers through his hair, holding him closer to her.

She pushed his shirt off his shoulders and down his arms. He tossed it aside. She wrapped her fingers around his arms, feeling the flexing of his fingers in his strong biceps. She brushed her lips over his shoulder, licking lightly at his skin. She loved the salty taste of his skin.

His hands were under her shirt, moving over her back and undoing her bra.

He pushed her shirt up over her head and tossed it on the floor, then peeled her bra down her arms. He skimmed his hand over her torso before lowering his mouth and suckling at her breast. She squirmed against him, reaching between their bodies to unfasten his pants. His cock was hot and hard under her touch. She rubbed him through his boxer shorts until he grunted deep in his throat and shifted to his side.

He kept one arm wrapped around her waist and his mouth at her breast. She caressed his length, teasing him with alternating light touches and squeezing caresses. Cupping his sac in her hands, she rolled his balls against her fingers and then brought her hand back up his erection.

She felt a drop of moisture at the tip and she rubbed her finger over it, smoothing it into him. She had never felt a man's cum hot and heavy on her body. She'd always had protected sex and no mistakes and she wondered what it felt like.

She continued to caress him with her hand until Kirk pulled back, taking her hand in his and holding it over her head. "I'm going to explode."

"Good," she said. "When we are like this I feel alive."

"You are alive and safe with me, Olivia."

His words made her pulse speed up and her center even wetter. She reached for the snap on her jeans, but Kirk's hands were already there, unfastening her pants and pushing them down her legs. She shivered at the feel of his hands on her legs, so close to her center.

He pulled a condom from the pocket of his pants and put it on. He draped her thighs over his arms and lowered himself over her, pushing her legs apart and entering her in one long thrust. She held on to his waist and felt the fire building inside her. It was the same fire that she'd felt before, but this time, now that she knew she wasn't fighting him as fiercely, it felt stronger, more intense.

This time, she didn't hide from what he made her feel. Instead she reveled in the feeling of being alive. Because she'd been sleeping for so long, going through the motions of pretending to be alive, she needed this moment. By trying to kill her, Ray had awakened her to the fact that she was finally taking control of her life.

There was a great freedom in knowing that she was in control. She pressed her face into Kirk's chest and breathed deeply. The scent of him made her feel so damned safe that she never wanted to forget it. She doubted she could ever explain to him just what he did to her. Beyond the sexual feeling he aroused in her, he found a way of making her life more complete.

That worried her because they were very different people who had led very different lives, and she didn't see how they were going to merge the two. She simply couldn't see him in a tuxedo at one of her parents' dinner parties.

But she could see him sitting on a couch in her flat, the two of them curled up enjoying their time together. And maybe that was enough, she thought.

For right now—it was.

Chapter Eighteen

Ray had his hands full answering questions from the authorities in Cullinan. They had been calling him to come down to the station since the day Olivia had disappeared.

"I don't have any information on a murder on the mining property," Ray said. Phillip and Lars were back at Onyx going through Ray's office, trying to figure out what records had been lost.

"Very well, sir, but the man who made the call said your fiancée had witnessed the crime."

"Are you aware that she was kidnapped that day?" Ray said. "I believe the man who made that call may be the person who is holding her hostage."

"Have you received a ransom notice?" Charity Keone-Williams asked. She had been hired by Olivia's parents to help with the investigation.

"No, we haven't," Ray said. "I don't think that Mrs. Keone-Williams is adding anything here, officer. She should wait outside."

"I'm sorry I can't do that. I am actually working with the police on this matter, Mr. Lambert."

He hated smartass women. "We haven't found any bodies on our property, so as far as the Onyx Diamond Group is concerned, there hasn't been any murder. We are concerned about a break-in last night in our corporate offices."

"We are looking into that. Your head of security," the officer looked down at his notes. "Mr. Jones, has supplied us with a security tape. Do you believe this is related to Ms. Pontuf's kidnapping?"

"Yes, I do. I had a look at the tape this morning and the man who assaulted Olivia's bodyguard appears to be the same man who kidnapped her at the airport."

Ray left the police station a few minutes later with Charity by his side. "I would like to accompany you back to the mining offices and see if I can help in your investigation."

Ray shook his head. "That's impossible. Diamond business isn't open to the outside. Please give my regards to Olivia's parents."

"I will," she said, pulling on a pair of dark sunglasses and walking away.

Charity was the kind of woman he usually found attractive—tall, very beautiful, and blond. But there was an edginess to her that he didn't like. She seemed to look right through him. He knew she couldn't possibly see beyond his guise of concern to the panicked man underneath.

His mobile rang and he answered it without looking at the caller ID. "Lambert here."

"Are you done at the police station?" Phillip asked.

"Yes. Why?"

"All of the missing files, according to your secretary, pertain to an abandoned mine. We want to go and inspect that area. Also we are shutting down production here until we can get control of these break-ins."

Ray balled his hand into a fist. "Don't make any rash decisions, Phillip. We've got the situation under control now. The problem was Thomas and he can't do any more damage to the mine."

"Thomas didn't break in here last night."

"I know that. I believe this is tied to the men who took Olivia. Obviously Thomas must have hidden something somewhere in the office building for them."

"Like what?" Phillip asked.

Ray had no idea. He needed time to think and come up with a plan. "I'm not sure. Let's keep the mine going until we have time to find out what's going on. I don't want to lose the production time."

"No one wants to see Onyx affected negatively by this, but we have to control our product."

"It is controlled. We aren't going to let anyone leave the property with as much as a fleck of diamond on them. I've doubled the security staff."

"We can discuss this when you get back out here. When can we expect you?"

"Thirty minutes tops," Ray said.

He walked to his car as he ended the call. He needed to get control of Phillip and Lars. He knew the other men would be driven to do what was necessary to keep the consortium happy, but he needed to keep the mine in production so that the diamonds he'd just sold didn't enter the market after Onyx closed down. That would raise too many questions.

Questions that would lead straight back to him. Because there was no way one man could have taken as many diamonds as Ray had sold to his men on the black market. And that would lead the consortium to the conclusion that he'd been dealing under the table.

* * *

Kirk left Olivia with Anna and joined the rest of the Savage Seven. They were all sitting around a table for six dressed in desert camo and T-shirts. He took his seat, but there was still one spot that was empty and they all were aware of the man who was missing.

"Burati told us that Lambert is on the verge of making a big deal with a black-market arms dealer. He's been supplying diamonds that the man uses to purchase guns."

"About damn time," Hamm said. Hamm was outspoken and a bit of a loudmouth most of the time, but Kirk agreed with him. They needed a break in the information they were getting if they were going to close this mission. Hamm was a thick-necked redhead who, like Kirk, had spent most of his life fighting.

Next to him was Van. Van was quiet and the smallest guy on their team. But he was savvy in an eerie kind of way about knowing how to get inside their enemies' heads. "It is about time. I think we can use this to our advantage. Kirk, can you use your network of black-market contacts to find who Lambert's buyer is?"

"Sure. I'll do it when we're finished here."

"How are we set for weapons and ammo?" Savage asked.

"I've already restocked on ammo for the team. We're ready for anything we encounter," Laz said.

Kirk put his hand on Laz's shoulder. "Anything they encountered," in Lazspeak, meant everything short of a nuclear attack. And even then Kirk wasn't too sure Laz wasn't prepared.

"Van, what'd you find out? Anything new at the police station?"

"Charity said that Lambert looked like he was sweating when the police questioned him. They aren't too sure whom to believe. It'd be great if the body of the person Olivia saw murdered turned up," Van said without glancing up from the computer in front of him.

"Do you want us to do a sweep of the area?" Kirk asked Savage, all the while mentally compiling a picture of the team's readiness. They fairly vibrated with the need to be moving.

"No. That body is gone and we'll probably never find it," Savage said. The important thing right now is to break Lambert. He's the threat to Olivia. And until we do we're not going to get out of here.

Kirk nodded. "This isn't our normal sort of job."

"No, it's not, but Olivia is a friend of Anna's, and we take care of friends," Savage said.

That made Kirk feel better. He knew he wasn't going anywhere until Olivia was safe and he wanted his guys at his back. Kirk's BlackBerry vibrated and he glanced at the screen to see he had a new e-mail. "I'm going to need to go meet one of my contacts."

"What about?" Savage asked.

"I put out a few feelers when we first got here to see if anyone had heard anything on the dead guy. One of my contacts has some information."

"How reliable is this source?" Savage asked. "Have you used them before?"

"Well I bought them, so I guess we can trust them as far as what I paid. He's an Afrikaaner who's got no love for Onyx Diamond Group."

South Africa was in a dangerous position, what with so many rebels still fighting for rights that Kirk wasn't too sure they'd ever get. The United States wasn't the favored son here, but then that was true of just about every country the Seven traveled to.

"I say we take the little bastard with us and if his intel is wrong . . ."

Kirk shook his head at Laz's comment. The men were tense, but not in a nervous way. They were ready for action. They wanted to do something instead of hanging out in this house and waiting for the intel they needed to move, and Kirk did as well.

"Kirk and Laz, go together to meet his contact. If the guy is trustworthy, pay him and then report back here," Savage said.

The group split up a few minutes later and Kirk went outside for a few minutes alone. Until Olivia he hadn't really thought much about the fact that he essentially did a young man's job. A job for the type of man who had nothing to lose and thought he'd never die. But Kirk's thinking had changed sometime over the last few days and he wasn't sure he liked it.

Sure, he liked what he had with Olivia, but she was the kind of woman he'd always pictured settled down. And he wasn't that type of guy.

"Kirk?"

"Yes, Wenz?" Kirk asked. Wenz rounded out their team as their medic. Each man had EMT training, but Wenz was their designated medic. The man had calm hands during the most intense firefight.

"Just wanted to check on that scrape you sustained as we were pulling out."

"It's fine. I bandaged it myself when we got back."

"You sure?" Wenz asked, but Kirk knew that the medic had something other than the injury on his mind. Lately he felt like it was going to take more than stubbornness to keep him alive. Olivia hadn't distracted him last night, but he felt she was weakening him.

And if she was, how was he going to deal with that?

Would he be like Savage, trading action and the thrill of pitting himself against an unknown enemy to sit back at the command center? Could he live like that? Would Olivia want him if he did?

He shook his head and forced his mind back to the mission and away from a woman who was more distraction than she should be.

He was focused on finding the information he needed to make Olivia safe. Then he could figure out the rest of this stuff. Right now his only concern was keeping her safe. That was all he could do. Later . . . if she wanted to continue seeing him, he'd figure out if he could live with her and continue to be used as a weapon.

The capital city of Johannesburg wore its new government influences well. But the signs of crime were still present in the graffiti and the barbed wire around the moneyed neighborhoods. Kirk rubbed the back of his neck as he ducked out of the busy foot traffic and into a McDonald's where he was to meet his contact.

This was the kind of city he always felt at home in because it wore its violence like a banner. There was a lot of war in this part of the world and he thought that this was more his home than anyplace where he might sleep back in the States.

Laz was down the street and connected to Kirk via their wireless earpiece/microphones.

No matter what he might want to believe, he knew that men like him had always been around and that fighting was something that had come naturally to this land in every age. There was something wild and untamed about South Africa that drew him. Something that made even the most determined atheist sense there was a higher force at play in this land.

Kirk ordered a Big Mac from the attendant in perfect Afrikaans. Most of the locals spoke that language. And he was dressed like a national. The disguise was hot and sticky and he couldn't help but remember the distance in Olivia's eyes as she'd seen him dressed like this.

He tried to shake off that feeling. He thought instead that no matter where he was in the world he could get a Big Mac, but there was still something a little weird about ordering one in a foreign language.

Kirk found a table in the back of the restaurant and sat down to wait for his contact. He reached in his bag of food to snag a fry, but the clerk yelled out to stop him.

"Wait, sir. That is the wrong bag."

Kirk pushed to his feet and handed the clerk the bag he'd been given. The new bag was slightly heavier and Kirk glanced inside to see a small yellow capsule nestled in with his supersized fries.

"Thanks," he said to the clerk and worked his way back out onto the street. The last time he'd had McDonald's fries had been in D.C. before they'd left on their mission to help Anna and Liberty Investigations capture a terrorist in Algeria.

There was something very American about the fries and he wished he could share them with Olivia. Maybe tasting something of home would give her that sense of normalcy she was searching for.

He wanted that for her. He needed to know she was safe. She wouldn't understand it and he wasn't ever going to let her know it—but she made what he did worthwhile. Knowing that she was safe while he saved the world, or at least a small portion of it, made it easier for him to sleep at night.

"My contact left a package for me," Kirk said.

"Great. I'm at the end of the street and going for the car," Laz said.

He pocketed the capsule and made his way out onto the street, blending into the throng of people. He moved slowly and carefully. Although he wanted to examine the information he'd been given, he knew he couldn't.

A late-model car pulled to a stop next to him. Kirk identified Laz quickly and slid into the car as Laz pulled away from the curb.

"How'd it go?"

"Smooth."

"Does anything ever not go smoothly for you?"

"Yes. But only temporarily," Kirk said. He had an image to keep up, especially around his men.

He palmed open the capsule and removed a tiny microdisc. He couldn't wait to get back and give this to Van, who was the team's computer expert and would be able to analyze it. "We should have brought a computer with us."

"This should be a satellite tape of the murder on the Onyx Mining grounds."

"Nice. Those rebels aren't as unsophisticated as the nightly news would have the world believe."

"No, they aren't. Drug dealers and weapons brokers are good for a thing or two."

"Until we have to go after them."

Kirk didn't take his eyes off the terrain. "That's not our mission this time."

"It'd be nice to have the upper hand a time or two," Laz said.

"Hell, yes it would be," Kirk said.

They left the city of Johannesburg and headed toward Pretoria. The lights of the city dropped away behind them as they rode out into the barren landscape. The night closed in around them as they sped along the highway. As they left the city, a round of fire ripped through the night. Laz kept on driving through the area and Kirk pulled his firearm and returned fire.

"Someone's following us."

"Who is it?" Kirk asked.

"One of the men from the mining company."

"Fuck. We can't lead them back to the safe house. We need to lose them."

"I'm doing my best."

Kirk didn't say anything else, just turned in the seat and kept his weapon trained on the other car. Laz turned off the lights, weaving through the traffic until they left the other car in the dust.

He pulled into a run-down neighborhood. "Let's leave the car here."

"Good idea."

He sent a text to Savage telling them they'd been hit and were coming in on foot.

He and Laz moved in sync, finding the natural cover provided by the neighborhood. They found a late-model sedan and Laz picked the lock and they climbed into the car. Laz had it up and running in no time. They pulled away from the curb and heard a man yelling at them.

But Laz just kept driving.

"I grew up in a neighborhood like this one," Kirk said.

"Did you? I grew up in a nice safe suburb," Laz said.

"Then why'd you turn to this life?" Kirk asked. Because if he'd grown up somewhere nice like Laz's childhood home, he'd never have wanted to leave it.

Laz laughed, but there was no mirth in the sound. "I wanted to make the world a better place. Try to give kids like the ones that live here," he gestured toward the row houses in the distance, "a chance at the good life."

Kirk nodded and didn't say anything else. That was part of the reason why he'd gotten into the Corps. That and the fact that a weapon needed to be used. And Kirk had always been a weapon.

Chapter Nineteen

Anna and Olivia had spent all day poring over the files and had compiled damning evidence that linked Ray to a group of known terrorists. Each new piece of information they had uncovered had made Olivia realize that Ray's trying to kill her had been the wake-up call that she'd needed. Getting out of his house was the best thing she could have done.

"Kirk and Laz are in trouble," Savage said, coming into the room where they were.

"What kind of trouble?" Olivia asked. She hadn't seen Kirk since this morning and she missed him. She hadn't thought she could grow so dependent on one man so quickly, but she had.

"I'm not sure. They had to ditch their vehicle. I sent Hamm to the car to see if anyone took interest in it."

"Is it safe for them to be on foot? Jo'burg after dark isn't the safest place," Olivia said. Then she realized who she was talking about. "Sorry. Of course they'll be fine. It's Jo'burg that should watch out."

"They can take care of themselves," Savage said.

Savage pulled Anna to the side to talk to her alone, and Olivia got up and walked to the window. She hated this place and how dangerous it was. This wasn't the first time she'd heard of a car being attacked that way. This place was just full of unrest.

How had she ever thought she could make a life here? Even with Kirk by her side, she doubted she'd ever feel safe enough to live here. She couldn't wait to get back to her civilized world. Manhattan or London. A big city where mugging was the biggest threat, not car shootings or kidnappings.

She knew location wasn't a guarantee of safety, but she'd feel better in the concrete jungles she knew—way safer than she felt here in this strange land with people she couldn't relate to.

"Olivia?"

"Hmm?"

"You okay?" Anna asked. Savage had left while she'd been standing there, Olivia realized.

"Fine, I guess. I'm having a tough time dealing with everything that has been happening. I mean, I was planning a wedding, and now I'm in hiding."

"That's completely understandable," Anna said.

"And . . . I don't want to make you uncomfortable, but I think I'm falling for Kirk."

Anna's eyes widened. "He's nothing like the men you normally date."

"You think I don't know that? I know that we don't make sense outside this situation, but I feel like there's a part of me that is very similar to him."

Anna came over and sat down next to her. "What part?"

"The loner part. You know, despite my social obligations I really like being alone, and I can tell Kirk does, too. He has this calmness . . . this quietness inside him that soothes me."

"It was like that for Savage and me. On the surface, I felt

like he was someone I'd never be able to accept or trust, but he is."

Olivia felt a lot better thinking about Anna. She might be the only woman who understood the relationship she was embarking on.

"Now that we have this information on Ray, what will you do with it? A part of me wants to confront him, make him admit that he's a scumbag," Olivia said.

"That would be satisfying, but we will take it to the officials and we'll have to contact someone from the diamond consortium. They will want to retrieve the diamonds that Ray sold. They only allow so many from each mine into the market each year," Anna said.

"I know. I hope that doesn't mean they'll shut down the mine in Cullinan. There are a lot of workers who rely on their jobs there."

Anna nodded. "We can try to influence them not to shut it down, but those men answer only to themselves."

"I know. They are like a dictatorship. Phillip is on the consortium and I know he still has to answer to the board. They follow very strict rules."

"They also have consequences for breaking the rules," Anna said.

"Like what?"

"I've heard they kill men who steal from them. So if Ray going to jail is important to you, we need to go to the cops first."

Olivia shook her head. "Why do men think it's okay to just kill?"

"It's not just men," Anna said. "The world is full of this gray area that most people don't realize exists. But courts can't necessarily regulate a fitting punishment in some places."

Olivia realized what her friend was saying and for a minute

she felt very naïve and stupid. "I guess South Africa is one of those places."

"Yes, it is. Here the diamond consortium has to be swift with their reactions when someone steals from them, otherwise everyone would try to do it. And then they'd lose the control they have over their product and their workers."

Olivia didn't like it. Didn't care for this world she'd only been on the outskirts of. She realized that, as much as she cherished her new knowledge and relationship with Kirk, she wanted to go back to not knowing this kind of stuff.

Kirk was tired and irritated by the time they got back to the safe house. He met with Savage and they had determined that they had enough information to have Lambert arrested, which was fine and dandy but he wasn't really a gathering-information-and-waiting guy.

No one on the team was, and they were ready for some kind of action. But there was none to be found here. Savage had another job lined up for them as soon as this one ended, in the Indian Ocean off Somalia, where pirates were preying on oil tankers, shipping freighters, and luxury boats.

Fighting pirates was exactly what Kirk needed. Today had just reinforced to him that there wasn't anything that could come out of his relationship with Olivia.

"What are we doing with Olivia?" Kirk asked.

"She is booked on a flight to London this afternoon. Her parents will meet her at the airport. Anna has worked with her contacts there to keep Olivia's arrival out of the media."

"That's good. She doesn't need that kind of attention," Kirk said. He had to say good-bye to her. He knew that. But this just made him realize that no matter what he'd been hoping for earlier, she wasn't going to be his.

"Who's taking her to the airport?" Kirk asked after a few minutes.

"Anna and I can do it if you don't want to."

Kirk looked at his boss and friend and realized the other man knew exactly what he was going through. "I'll do it. Where is the team meeting up to move on?"

"Freight airport. Laz got us a Blackhawk."

"How?"

"I have no idea. That boy is magic when it comes to making things happen," Savage said. "You know, you have time off coming to you. If you want to take a week and go to London no one would say anything."

Kirk shook his head. "I can't do that."

"Don't let a good thing slip away," Savage said.

"I'm not. You've just become domesticated."

Savage looked like he was going to argue, but then just shrugged. "Have I?"

"Hell, yes," Kirk said.

"Looking for a fight?"

Kirk nodded. "But not now."

"Why don't you hit the gym?" Savage suggested.

"I might. Hamm said that the car was gone by the time he got to it, so we won't know if it's related to the diamond lies that Lambert has been juggling."

"It felt random to me. I don't think they know where we are or even who we are," Savage said.

"I agree."

Anna came into the room and walked over to Savage. She wrapped her arms around his shoulders and lowered her head to kiss her husband. "I'm glad you are back safely, Kirk. Olivia's upstairs if you are looking for her."

"Why would I be looking for her?"

"No reason," Anna said.

Kirk felt like a jerk talking to Anna that way. "Sorry."

She smiled at him. "It's fine."

Savage looked like he didn't necessarily agree. Kirk decided it was time to get out of there.

"Later."

He climbed the stairs, feeling every one of his thirty-seven
years. And his soul . . . so weighted down with all the kills
he'd taken over the years. He knew then that Olivia was making him feel this way.

He wanted to come to her a young man with dreams and a
clean soul and instead he knew that he never could. Letting
her go was the only thing he could do. It was the only way that
they would both be able to live and not be disappointed.

He went to the room she'd been staying in and found the
door opened. She was obviously ready to go. He should just
grab a shower and go back with his team. Pretend he'd never
held her in his arms as his own. But he heard the sound of running down the hall.

Olivia put on her running shoes and workout clothes and
went to the gym. She was tired of waiting. She felt if she had
to sit in one of the rooms downstairs for another minute she'd
start screaming and God knows she didn't think she could
stop.

She had to wrap her ankle in an Ace bandage, but then she
felt like it was strong enough to withstand her running on it.
She really wanted to be outside. To just breathe the night air
and find that part of her center that she'd lost.

Anna had told her that the team had enough information to
have Ray arrested and it was time for her to safely return to
her parents in London. She was glad to get out of here, but
she was going to miss Kirk.

She got on the treadmill and ran away from the thoughts in
her head. Just focused on the poster on the wall that was a
tribute to Shakespeare's quotes.

She wished she had the freedom to just do what she

wanted. Instead she had to deal with the knowledge that be-cause she'd witnessed Ray doing something he shouldn't have been doing, many lives were in danger. Hers, Ray's, Kirk's, Anna's, her parents'.

That was a heavy burden and one she just didn't know if she could handle. She knew she was weak and she wondered if that was why she'd always enjoyed writing so much.

The world on the page was so much easier to control than the world she lived in. There were no hard-and-fast rules in the game they were playing with Ray and the dangerous men he dealt with on the black market.

There was no guarantee that things would work out the way she wanted them to. Instead she had to deal with the fact that there was a very strong possibility that this might never be fixed the way she wanted it to.

"Olivia?" Kirk called from the hallway.

"In here," she said, hitting the stop button and getting off the treadmill.

Kirk came in a minute later. He had several days' growth of stubble on his face and his hair had been colored darker than his normal shade. He seemed tired to her and she realized that he hadn't slept last night when she had. She should give him the peace and solace he gave her.

She walked over to him and took his hand in hers. "How are you? Savage said you had car trouble."

"Fine. I got some information from my contact that shows Lambert killing that man out at the mines."

"Good," she said, but she didn't want to talk about that now. "Do you have to be anywhere now?"

He gave her an odd look. "I don't think so. Why?"

She bit her lip at how needy that question made her sound. "Never mind. I don't know what I was thinking."

"Actually, we have about four hours until we are moving out to go and apprehend Lambert."

"I could use a shower."

"Good," she said. "You go get in the shower and I will get you something to eat."

"Thanks," he said. She started to walk away, but he stopped her with both hands on her waist. "I need a kiss first."

She turned in his arms and went up on her tiptoes kissing him before walking away, but he stopped her. "Forget the food. Let's shower together."

She nodded and followed him back to the bedroom where they'd spent most of their time together. They bathed and as they were drying off she realized this was the last time she'd be with him like this.

With a soft cry, Olivia wrapped herself around Kirk's warm body and didn't want to open her eyes. She just curled closer to him, resting her head on his chest right over his heart. His heart beat under her ear and she kept her eyes closed, not ready to move on. She knew this was the last time she'd be in his arms. Soon she was going to walk away from him and he was going to let her go.

She curled her arms around his chest as she felt his hands sweep down her back and draw her more fully against his body.

Kirk was the kind of man who could make her feel safer than anyone else ever had, but she knew that was a crutch and she had to figure out how to stand on her own because he had his own life. She'd been falling for him since the moment he'd rescued her from Burati.

His hand tightened on her ass and she lifted her head, looking down at him. He watched her with an intense awareness that made her suspect he might already know more about what was going on in her head than she wanted him to.

"Kirk—"

"No more talking. We both know this is it and I need to be inside you one more time."

He wrapped his hand around the back of her neck and drew her down toward him. His mouth opened lazily on hers and tasted the words that she was trying to get out. She forgot all about talking as he rolled her under his body and covered her completely.

Safety and security swamped her as he wrapped his arms around her, rocked his mouth over hers, and settled himself between her legs. It was too easy to read the expression in his eyes. Too easy to acknowledge that he wasn't letting her go without leaving his mark on her.

He cupped her head in his hands, rubbing his lips over hers and then licking a trail down the side of her neck to a spot just at the base of her neck. He sucked on her skin until she arched into him, wanting, searching for more from him. He lifted his head; his lips were full, swollen from all the kisses they'd shared.

He brushed his thumb back and forth over her lower lip until she bit on the tip of it and sucked it into her mouth. He continued his trail of licking and suckling kisses down to her breasts. He kissed her everywhere, didn't leave one inch of her torso unexplored. She was so sensitized from his kissing, she felt like she was going to explode.

Her nipples were tight buds and her breasts felt too full. He scraped his teeth up and down the sides of her breasts and then cupped her breasts in both his hands. He massaged her entire breast with his fingers and his palm.

She scraped her nails down his back, lingering at the scar on his hip. Her fingers moved over it and she remembered the stories he'd told her about his scarred body and the sacrifices he'd made to live his life by his own code. She looked into his gray eyes, which were anything but cold right now. She skimmed her hand around his hip to his cock, taking it in her hand and stroking him from base to tip.

She circled her finger over the tip at the end of each upstroke. Bracing himself with his arm, he levered up to give her greater access to his body. She loved the way he responded so openly to her caresses. He made love to her like she was the only woman in the world he wanted.

She skimmed her fingers into her own wetness and rubbed it on his erection. She kept caressing him until she felt a spurt of moisture at the tip of his cock. She caught it with her fingers, drawing her hand up to her mouth and licking her finger.

He bent down and opened his mouth over hers. Their tongues tangled, the mingled taste of both of their bodies in her mouth. He lowered himself over her again.

He continued his downward journey on her body, skimming his lips over her ribs and then tracing the line of each one with his tongue.

She couldn't get enough of him, though she'd never say it out loud. He made her feel so wonderfully safe. Like she was the most beautiful woman in the world. Like she had no flaws and was perfect the way she was. Not anyone else's version of perfect, just the perfect Olivia.

He lingered over her belly button, glancing up at her over the length of her body. She swallowed hard and pulled him back up over. She reached out blindly for the condom packet on the nightstand and grabbed one, tearing it open and fitting it over him in one smooth motion.

He tested her with his fingers and then shifted his hips and entered her in one smooth movement. She held on to his hips, urging him to be still when he would have started thrusting. Their gazes met and held and she took a deep breath, so that the mingled scents of their skin and sex were embedded deep in her senses as he made love to her for the last time. She never wanted to forget this moment, she thought.

The softness of the mattress beneath her back and the hardness of his body over hers. When he started to thrust she lifted her hips to meet his. Slid her hand down between their bodies and caressed his balls with her fingers. Then slipped her hand a little lower, pressing on his perineum. His hips jerked harder against her. He reached down, pulling her hand away from him.

He pushed her legs back against her own body to give him greater access to her. His thrusts were fiercer now and she couldn't do anything but hold on to his hips and let the feelings he generated wash over her.

Every nerve in her body convulsed as her orgasm raced through her. He only grunted her name and changed the angle of his penetration, riding her hard through her climax until she felt it build again. It was too much. She couldn't do it again. She wanted to slide down on the bed and close her eyes, but he was relentless, using his cock, his mouth, his hands to build her once again toward the pinnacle and this time following her over.

Her orgasm was even more intense than the first. He called her name as he emptied himself into her, collapsing against her chest. She wrapped her arms around his shoulders, one hand in his hair as he rested his face between her breasts. His breath sawed in and out of his open mouth, warming her chest and sending goose bumps all over her highly sensitive skin.

He glanced up at her and she tried to close her eyes and look away. Tried to give herself a place to hide. But she knew it was too late for that.

He cupped her face in his hands and kissed her with exquisite tenderness that rocked her body and soul. She clung to him even though she didn't want to. She held him closer to her, wrapping her arms and legs around his body as the sweat dried on his back.

They both got up and dressed in silence, not saying anything until Olivia realized that if she let him, he'd leave without a word.

And that was the last thing she wanted. She hadn't told him

that she loved him and that she wanted to figure out a way to have a life with him once they were both out of this mess.

This mess . . .

This was her life. She was going to be starting over from scratch and she realized that she wanted to start over with Kirk, but that wasn't going to happen. How was she going to survive without him? They were sending her back to London to meet her parents, but she didn't want to go. She was afraid to leave this house in South Africa.

But she had no idea if Kirk wanted a life with her. Had he been interested in her for anything other than sex?

She'd like to hope so, but it was hard to tell. Because they had been thrown together in this situation. This life where nothing was real and tension and adrenaline were the only things she could count on.

She went to the hallway, but it was empty. She needed to talk to Kirk one more time, but she knew all of a sudden that she wasn't going to get that chance.

And she wanted to cry. She felt a bit like a coward for letting him slip away like that.

When was she going to be able to let go of her fears and trust a man again? She didn't care about any other man except for Kirk. She needed to be able to trust him, because he already owned her heart.

Chapter Twenty

Ray was beyond pissed off when he saw Phillip, Lars, and two uniformed Cullinan police officers walk into his office. This wasn't the way the diamond consortium had been rumored to handle illegal activities.

"Mr. Lambert is very busy," Anita was saying, trying to keep the men out of his office.

"I'll have to ask you to leave," Burati said, standing up and blocking the door.

"What is going on here?" Ray asked Lars.

"We have evidence that you have been working two abandoned mine shafts after hours," Lars said. "It's not what we wanted to do, but you know that the system is in place and we have to follow our own rules."

Ray nodded. He had thought over the last few days that Lars had started to side with him. "I didn't condone any mining in those shafts."

"I'm sorry, Ray, but we have voice and video recordings of you doing so," Phillip said. "Officers, please arrest him."

The officers moved forward to do so and Ray felt his temper

boil over. Just who the hell did Phillip think he was? Lars was the company man who'd gone over to the consortium. Lars was the only one he had to answer to.

Ray looked directly at the other man. "Don't do this."

"My hands are tied. I'm afraid Phillip and the other board members have decided on this course of action."

At least that told Ray where this was coming from. "Phillip, I know you are upset because your cousin is missing—

"It's more than that. There have been rumors about you for years—about the way you have used and abused your workers. We are trying to be a more internationally aware organization and we can't be when men like you are in charge."

"Men like me? You mean men who can run an organization and turn a profit?" Ray asked.

Phillip walked over to him and leaned over the desk. "No, I mean men who still think that they are some sort of demigod instead of realizing they are simply managing directors."

The officers stepped around his desk on either side, and Ray shook his head as he stood up. He held his wrists out to the men and he was cuffed. "You will regret this once I've talked to my lawyer."

"If you can prove otherwise—that you aren't the man I believe you to be—then I will apologize," Phillip said.

"Is this about Olivia? I told you I know nothing about her disappearance," Ray said.

"We have evidence that you tried to kidnap her. She is in the hands of someone who has protected her until you are in jail."

Ray was led out of his office past workers who seemed stunned. He was humiliated and upset. And as he was force-marched down to the police car, he realized there was one person to blame for this mess.

Olivia.

If she hadn't disappeared, then Phillip wouldn't have come here and paid so much attention to everything.

As soon as he was in the car with the men Ray started talking to them, offering them money and anything else they wanted. It was the money that did it. They drove him to his house in Sandton instead of to the station and he paid the men handsomely for their decision.

He would go to the airport and get out of the country. He called Monte, who had taken care of all his transactions involving illegal uncut diamonds.

"What can I do for you today?"

"I need a new identity and new money. I have to get out of Jo'burg tonight."

"I will see what I can do, but it will cost you."

"I have money," Ray said. That was the one thing he did have. Beyond the Swiss account that Olivia had taken the bankbook for. He really wanted to get his hands on Olivia. He was lucky that the men at the police department had been bribable. But he knew that the government authorities wouldn't be as easy as the local cops had been.

For a moment he wondered if he should just leave South Africa and not deal with Olivia. But she'd cost him. It turned out she'd cost him everything and that kind of action had to be dealt with. So he would make her pay.

Olivia walked through the crowded airport, feeling a profound sense of shock that everything had changed so much in five short days. She couldn't believe she was back at the airport, this time without Kirk.

Savage and Anna had gone with her to the ticket counter, but everyone seemed to be of the same mind-set, that there was nothing more to worry about. She felt a sense of relief as she collected her ticket and then stepped away from the desk to find Anna. Kirk and Savage were standing in an open area not too far away and they looked out of place.

She bumped into a man as she turned. He was taller than she was and his cologne was familiar. She glanced up with a smile on her face, thinking it must be someone she knew, and was shocked to realize it was Ray.

She screamed and tried to pull away from him, but he held her arm tightly in his grip. "Don't make a scene, darling."

She opened her mouth to scream again, but he brought his mouth down on top of hers before she could make a sound. She tried struggling and pulling away from him, but he kept her close and fast.

She tried to bite his lip or tongue, but he brought his free hand up to her neck and squeezed threateningly. He lifted his mouth from hers. "Don't make me hurt you, Olivia. If you come with me, the man who took you will live."

"What man?"

"Kirk, I believe his name is," Ray said.

She glanced around the airport lobby area and saw Kirk and Savage both running toward her.

Ray saw them, too, and dragged her through the crowds into a large tour group. She looked back, but she couldn't see anyone. Not Anna or Savage or Kirk or any of the other guys from the Savage Seven.

"I thought you were going to be arrested," she said.

"Not yet, darling," he said, leading her toward the exit.

Olivia knew she had to stall, had to slow Ray down, and Kirk would rescue her. "Let me go, Ray."

He stopped and took her chin in his hand. "No. You owe me, Olivia. And you are going to pay."

"I owe you? Burati tried to kill me. No doubt on your orders. Since you would have when I drove by you if my car didn't have bulletproof glass."

"Very true."

"Did you ask me to bring the envelope out there so you could do that?"

"No," he said. "It is unfortunate that Thomas was caught that day. I was looking forward to our marriage, Olivia."

"Why?"

"I like you," he said.

She doubted that. "How could you kill me, then?"

"You are one of those people who can't look the other way when there is something wrong, and I had no choice but to get rid of you. My business depends on it."

"Your business?" she asked. "Ray, you make a very good living as a managing director."

"It wasn't enough. But that doesn't matter now. I'm on the run, thanks to you, and I've decided that your family will pay ransom for you."

"Why? Why not just make a run for it?" she asked. "I'll give you all the money I have."

"It's not enough. I'm going to have to start over from scratch."

"What are you doing with me?"

He led her out into the hot afternoon sun and across the parking lot to the parking garage. She struggled, but now that they were away from other people he simply punched her in the stomach, which made pain explode in her body. She stopped struggling.

As they approached Ray's car, a tall black man walked toward them. He took Olivia's hands from Ray and held her in tightly. "What are we going to do with her?"

"Put her in the trunk. Tie her hands and make sure that she can't escape."

"Please don't do this, Ray. I will give you whatever money you need. Just leave me here."

"It's too late to use that account. Your cousin Phillip had the account frozen. I have nothing left, Olivia."

"Yes, you do. Don't think like that," she said, digging her feet and trying to pull free.

"Stop it. Or I'll break your wrists."

"Please don't do that," she said.

"Shut her up, someone is coming," Ray said. Olivia felt the black man's hand on her neck and then she slowly lost consciousness.

Olivia woke with a start. Dull pain throbbed at the base of her neck and her stomach felt like one big bruise. She heard nothing but the loud sound of a ticking clock and the shuffle of footsteps over the cement pavement.

She opened her eyes as little as possible, trying to figure out the best way to take control of her current situation. Her hands were bound behind her back and she tried working at the thick stiff bindings. And she was on the floor of a car. It felt smooth on one side, rough on the other. Maybe a leather belt?

Her feet were bound, and a handkerchief was stuffed in her mouth. She worked her jaw carefully, using her tongue to push the cloth out of her mouth. Her head ached bad enough that she could hear her own racing heartbeat echoing in her head.

She couldn't wait around to be rescued. No one knew she'd been taken. She was scared and afraid and had no idea what to do next. Especially since she knew time was running out. She'd figure this out.

She steadily worked her hands against their bonds, knowing that nothing other than slow and steady movements would work to free her.

Olivia pushed herself into a sitting position. And felt her stomach rebel.

"Good. You're awake."

Startled, she brought her face around to the left and for the first time noticed the man sitting there. He was the big black man who'd taken her from Ray. He had on chinos and a plaid button-down shirt.

She tried to speak, but felt bile well up in her throat and she turned away, throwing up. She shook and felt moisture on her face. The man didn't move, just sat there staring at her. She wiped her face on her shoulders.

The front door opened and Ray got in the car. "I don't think I was followed. Is she awake?"

"Yes, I am. Let me go, Ray. This is just silly. If the diamond consortium knows you've been stealing from them, you know they won't let you get away with it."

"That's why I have you, Olivia. You are my insurance policy."

"Get up front, Taji," Ray said. "I don't want anyone thinking I'm your driver."

Taji opened the door and Olivia heard the sound of footsteps. She dragged herself toward the open door and stuck her head out the opening.

"Help me!" she screamed. "Please help!"

Taji lifted his foot and she was afraid he was going to kick her in the head. She dug her feet into the floor of the car and pushed with all her might. She hit the pavement hard as she spilled out of the car. Taji grabbed her and held her in front of his body.

He kept his hand over her mouth, strangling her cries. She heard Ray start to run and then felt the man behind her flinch and a splatter of blood hit the side of her face.

She felt like she was going to pass out as the man crumpled at her feet. His eyes were wide open, but he was dead from a bullet in the head.

She looked around, but Ray was in his car. He fired his own weapon out the window in the direction the shot had come from as he drove by.

Olivia was shaking and alone as she saw the silhouette of a

man walking toward her. He held a long rifle type gun in his right hand and he moved in a way that was achingly familiar to her.

That confident walk and long stride belonged to only one man. "Kirk."

She started running toward him, and he caught her up with one hand. She noticed the rest of the Savage Seven were behind them. The men she'd last seen relaxed and smiling were serious now, deadly serious as they bagged the body of the man who'd held her.

Wenz gave her an antiseptic wipe and she used it to clean the blood from her own face. Kirk hadn't said anything to her and that was fine. She'd realized when she'd looked in his eyes that he wasn't going to walk away from her again. Or, rather, she wasn't going to let him.

She needed him and there was noplace in the world she'd ever feel safe without having him by her side.

"How did Ray find me?" she asked Savage.

"He bribed the arresting officer and escaped."

"He's crazy now. He feels like he has nothing left to lose."

"Oh, but he does," Kirk said.

"What?" she asked, chilled by his monotone voice. This was the man she loved but he wasn't acting like she had expected him to. She could tell that he'd changed, and she had no idea what had caused the change in him.

She looked over at him, hoping that eye contact would show her Kirk's gentler side, but he wasn't in the mood to soothe her fears right now. He was in full-out warrior mode, she realized.

"His life."

Burati waited until after the cops had taken Ray away and Lars had left to talk freely to Phillip.

"I'm not sure that was the best idea," Burati said. "He still has connections in the police force."

"I know that. But we had to make a move on him. He was almost impossible to frame here. Now he'll either go to jail and stay there or break the law in such a way that we can take care of him."

Burati realized that the diamond consortium wasn't going to allow Ray Lambert to simply go to jail for his crimes. They wanted him to pay and with his entire life.

"What should I do?"

"For now, get to the station and try to get him released. It's important he still believe you are loyal to him."

Burati left the offices a bit shaken. He'd thought he was working for the better of two men, but now he was coming to realize he worked for the lesser of two evils. And that was hard to stomach.

His mobile beeped and he glanced down at the text screen. Ray was free of the cops already.

Burati had seen the anger in the other man's face and knew that Lambert's first course of action would be to get new papers and to take care of Olivia. Over the last day and a half, Lambert had started talking about how she was the one thing that had cost him everything.

Without a second thought, Burati dialed Kirk Mann's mobile.

"Mann here."

"It's Burati. I'm not with Lambert, so I can't be certain, but I know he is going to the airport. Make sure Olivia isn't there."

"What? How did he get away from the cops?"

"He is angry. He will kill her if he gets the chance," Burati answered. Today was the day when they had been planning to go and find her in the city.

"Thanks for the warning. I've got to go."

Mann disconnected the call and Burati sat in his car for a long moment. He knew he had to keep working for Lambert. As he drove back to Sandton, he realized that he didn't mind that. That he was ready to become the man that Phillip wanted him to be. Because working for the consortium was what he wanted.

Burati drove toward Soweto, up and down the streets lined with cardboard-box houses. He sat in his car, parked in the area where he'd grown up.

He had always believed that in order to move forward sometimes a man had to look back. And looking back always convinced him to keep his head on straight.

He wasn't going to take any chances with anyone else. He needed to keep working for the consortium because he didn't want to be back here.

He wanted a wife and some children of his own. He wanted what he'd seen of Lambert's white-world life. He wanted to know that if he got married and his wife was lucky enough to get pregnant that their baby wouldn't be born with HIV or another disease.

He needed to believe that he was a better man than his father had been so he could provide a future for the next generation of Buratis.

And as he started the car up and drove to meet Ray Lambert, he realized that he was probably going to always have to do work for men he could barely tolerate.

Because men like Burati were always going to have to find a way to make the white man's world work for him. Despite the new government that was in place, he'd learned a long time ago that there was always one class who made the rules and everyone else had to follow them.

Chapter Twenty-one

AUGUST 5, JOHANNESBURG

K irk was icy with rage as he sat in the back of the Humvee following the tracking signal they'd managed to embed in the bumper of Lambert's car two days ago thanks to Burati's help. Hamm and Van had done it while he and Laz had been picking up the information from his contact.

Kirk retreated into himself. They had to go to the police station and report the man he'd killed. He didn't like that because it would slow them down and give Lambert an even bigger lead on them. And right now all Kirk wanted was that man dead.

But he knew that wasn't the way to approach a job like this. He was too emotional.

Damn. How had that happened? He was never emotional about kills. Olivia sat huddled in the seat next to him and he reached over to take her hand in his. She clung to his hand, holding him so tightly that he could almost not believe it.

He leaned down and kissed her lightly above her ear.

"You saved me again," she said. Her eyes were so large in that pale face of hers.

"I know."

"Why are we going to the police?" she asked.

"Because Kirk isn't allowed to just kill someone and walk away. Since we aren't here to do that, we have to report it. We also want to talk to the officer in charge of arresting Lambert and find out what the hell went wrong," Savage said.

"Where's Anna?"

"She was waiting for you at your gate. I sent her to London to meet with your parents and to keep an eye on them. Charity is already on her way there as well."

"Thank you," Olivia said. She was shaking a little. "Do you think my parents are in danger? Ray wanted to ransom me."

"That's not going to happen," Kirk said.

"I meant to have Anna show me some self-defense moves, but then I figured I didn't need to know any."

"Kick him in the balls," Laz said. "That'll slow him down next time."

"We heard you scream at the airport. Good job," Kirk said.

She lifted her hand to her mouth and he noticed for the first time how swollen her mouth was. "He kissed me and bit my lip and said all kinds of threatening things."

"What kind of things?" he asked.

She turned her head up to his. "He said he'd kill you, Kirk."

Kirk let go of her hand and put his arm around her shoulders hugging her close to his side. "No one is going to kill me. Certainly not a little bastard like Ray Lambert."

"Everyone can be killed," she whispered.

"Not me. I'm indestructible," he said.

She smiled then. Her pale face took on a pretty rosy flush. He rubbed his lips lightly over hers to keep from hurting her. "I almost died when he said they'd kill you."

"We'll talk when this is over. But don't you worry about

THE MERCENARY   199

anything. I'm going to personally see that we both get out of this alive."

"What about your assignment? You all were supposed to leave this afternoon."

"Savage postponed it. We are going to finish off Lambert first," Kirk said. He really wanted to finish the man off. He was the scum of the earth as far as Kirk was concerned and he wanted to ensure he'd never again lay his hands on Olivia.

"So you'll have to leave as soon as this over to go to your next job?" Olivia asked.

"We can talk about that as soon as we get Lambert behind bars," Kirk said.

They were almost to the police station. "You'll have to stay in the Humvee with Laz and the guys. Just Savage and I will go in. Don't leave the vehicle for any reason. Not to pee or get a drink of water. Nothing, understand?" Kirk asked.

"Yes, I understand. What do you think will happen at a police station?"

"I don't know, but I'm not taking any chances. And as of now I'm in charge of you, Olivia. Until we know Lambert is neutralized, you got it?"

"Yes," she said, "Just make sure you take care with yourself, too. I won't be happy if you get hurt."

"I will be fine," he said. They pulled up in front of the police department. Savage got out and Kirk followed him. He had his sniper rifle in its case. He wasn't too concerned about this meeting. It was a minor irritation keeping him from getting to Lambert and making sure that bastard never touched Olivia again.

"I need to call my parents," Olivia said as they waited in the Humvee for Kirk and Savage to return. The waiting was excruciating, and she feared that Savage would come back without Kirk.

"Go ahead. We'll give you some privacy," Van said. He moved to the seat behind her, leaving her in the middle seat alone.

She dialed her mom's number and her mother answered on the first ring. "Livy?"

"Yes, mom. It's me."

"Thank God. Where are you?"

"Still in Johannesburg. I don't know how much you know, but Ray tried to kill me to cover up his illegal activities."

"We know, dear. Charity Keone-Williams has been here with us and explained everything. We thought you were returning to London."

"I will be, but not today. Ray tried to kidnap me again. He's going to send you a ransom note. Don't give him any money."

"We won't, Livy. Daddy wants to talk to you," Mom said.

"Are you okay, Livy?"

"Yes, Daddy. I'm fine. Anna and her company were great."

"See, I told you boarding school was the way to go. If you hadn't gone there you wouldn't have had Anna to turn to," her father said.

"You're right. Have you spoken to Phillip?"

"Yes, we called him as soon as Ray told us you'd been taken. He was very upset with Ray. I think Ray is going to lose his job."

"He's probably going to go to jail, Dad. He's been selling diamonds on the black market, which Phillip and the rest of the diamond consortium don't like."

"I never trusted that man," her father said.

"Is that true? I wasn't sure about him, but he seemed like a good catch."

"There is more to a good man than being a good catch," her dad said.

"Believe me, I know that now."

"I bet you do. When will we see you?"

"Soon, Daddy. I'll call when I can. I love you."

"We love you, too, Livy."

She hung up with her parents. The men in the vehicle with her all sat watching the world outside. She had noted they each had a weapon in their laps and all were ready to defend the Humvee.

"What's taking so long?" she finally asked when she couldn't stand the silence any longer.

Laz laughed and turned to look at her. "Who knows? It's never a quick trip when you have to explain a shooting to the authorities."

"I guess not. But with your backgrounds—"

"That just makes it worse," Hamm said.

"Why?" she asked. Hamm unnerved her. He was big and didn't say much and every time she looked at him she had the feeling he thought that she was a waste of their time and talents.

"Because Kirk isn't like your little criminal fiancé. He's done a laundry list of things that this government might not approve of. Or a government that is friendly with this one. So they might decide to hold him or deport him."

"Then why is he in there?" she asked.

"To make you happy, Missy."

"My name's not Missy," she said. "And I don't want him to be arrested."

"Of course not, but you want him to be a better man," Hamm said.

"I've never said that."

"You don't have to—that's what all women want."

"Maybe you don't know everything about women, Hamm. Because that's not what I want."

"There's no maybe about it, Olivia," Laz said. "Hamm's track record with the ladies is dismal."

"Like you're the ladies' man," Hamm said with a sneer.

"I do okay," Laz said, winking at Olivia.

Then he sat up and started the car. "Look alive, boys. Savage and Kirk are coming our way."

Olivia strained to see out the window, very happy to see Kirk coming back to her. She hadn't realized how much she loved him until today. It wasn't the fact that he'd saved her that had caused her knowledge but the fact that she realized she'd rather die then have him be killed.

He opened the door and climbed into the vehicle on one side while Savage got in on the other. She was sandwiched between the two men as Laz put the car in gear and they started driving away from the police station.

"How'd it go?" Hamm asked.

"As expected. They let us go but warned us to be careful about the amount of casualties."

"Did you say anything about their Mayberry buffoon cops letting Lambert escape?" Hamm asked.

Olivia had wondered about that, too.

"We did. They are investigating the entire affair. It seemed like they wanted to hold us longer, but I asked Sam to call the State Department and help us out. So they couldn't," Savage said.

Kirk had been quiet the entire time and when she reached over to touch him, he flinched away from her. She wondered what was going on in his mind.

She hated being surrounded by all these men. She needed to be alone with Kirk to talk to him. She realized he'd never open up to her the way he did when they were alone. Not in front of the group. He was the quiet loner in the group, and he didn't want anyone to see the man he revealed to her.

It didn't take a rocket scientist to figure that one out. She crossed her arms over her chest. "Where to now?"

"We think that Lambert is buying a new identity. We are going to head there and see if we can capture him."

"How do you know that?" Olivia asked.

"Because one of his black-market guys is a friend of mine," Kirk said.

"Aren't those men black-market gun dealers?" she asked.

"Yes. And my friend—Monte—set up a meeting with Lambert so we could apprehend him."

"Why would he do that?" Olivia asked.

"Monte has no loyalty except to the men who pay him. I've made it worth his while to help us out this time."

Olivia didn't like the sound of that. "What if Ray pays him more?"

"That's always a risk you run. But that's what the black market is about."

"What is? And how come it is so easy to find the 'black market' here?"

"Because there is no controlled exchange rate for money, men came up with a market to barter for local currency and that's how the black market started."

"Isn't it illegal?"

"Yes, Olivia, it is, but sometimes that's the only way to operate. At least here in South Africa it is."

"But you deal with this kind of thing wherever you are, don't you?" she asked. Trying to get a better handle on what it was he did. The glimpses she'd seen of the mercenary life were enough to scare her.

"Yes, I do. But it's that knowledge that has saved your life and kept you safe."

"I realize that," she said.

Chapter Twenty-two

Kirk had been in South Africa long enough to know the good neighborhoods from the bad ones. And the one where Monte had set up the deal between Lambert was one of the worst. No one came into that area unless they were fully armed.

They were all sitting around a table at Chancellor's Court, a guest home that was large and spacious and catered to families and groups normally. They'd rented the entire place for the night.

Kirk and the other men were in desert camouflage. They had a map of the area where they were going to set the trap for Lambert. Monte had been specific that he'd only do it for the money and he wouldn't wait around. He also couldn't and wouldn't guarantee anyone's safety.

Savage would be in the command vehicle this time and they were using satellite thermal heat images to determine who was in the area before they went in.

It was time for their in-briefing before the men moved forward with their mission. Savage also had to make sure they understood the rules of engagement. Savage had been emphatic that he didn't want to come and clean up a Rambo-style bloodbath.

"We'll go in quiet and quick," Savage said, restating their mission objective while Laz dispensed wireless radio earpieces to each of them. "Kirk will provide cover from here."

He indicated an apartment building that overlooked the corner where the meeting was to take place.

"Wenz, did you notice any gangs operating in the area?" Savage asked.

Wenz had been dispatched to the neighborhood to get a feel for it while Kirk had been scouting for a good sniper location.

"At least two warring factions. The entire neighborhood is a powder keg of violence and trouble. If we are quick, we should be able to slip in and out of the neighborhood without stirring up any other trouble."

"I think we should take them out. So we don't have to worry about them," Kirk said.

Kirk felt the tension in this group. They wanted Lambert out of the picture. As much as they hadn't wanted to be on bodyguard duty for Olivia, no one had expected her to be kidnapped under their noses, and they wanted to prove to her and to themselves that it wouldn't happen again.

They'd been waiting all day for action and now they were ready to move. Kirk was, too. He wanted everyone safe and then he wanted to take his leave so he could convince Olivia to be with him. The smoother and quicker they could get this done the better it would be for all involved.

"We're going in soft," Savage said to his men.

He looked at Kirk. "You need a confirmation before you make a kill—especially if it's Lambert. Is that understood?"

"Yes, sir."

"Let's check our radios and then we'll move out." Savage

waited until he was sure each man had placed an earbud in his ear.

"This is One," Kirk said.

"Two," Van said.

"Three," Laz said.

"Four," Wenz said.

"Five," Hamm said.

"And I'm Six," Savage said.

"We'll be on silent until we reach the target. Wenz, I want you to come in from the north side and take care of the sentry patrolling on that side."

Olivia would be in the vehicle with Laz. Leaving her behind this time hadn't been an option.

"Laz, you cover us from the west with the vehicle. Van and Hamm, you'll take the east and cover the road leading into the neighborhood."

"Let's move out."

The men all got up from the table and headed out to the vehicle. Kirk stayed behind, needing to check on Olivia one more time. "Ready to roll?"

"Yes. I think I am."

He led her down the hall to the waiting Humvee they were still using. Laz drove them through the streets of Pretoria to the square formed by Vermeulen, Du Toit, Boom, and Schubert Streets.

Kirk got out before the other men and ran swiftly to the apartment building where he'd set up for his shot. He got into position and set up his weapon. It felt like a lifetime since he'd been in another gutted apartment waiting to take a shot, he thought.

In a way it had been, because he was no longer the man he had been.

He saw the other men fanning out in the area surrounding

the square. The moon had risen and was full, giving them too much exposure as they maneuvered through the streets. They were on silent maneuvers tonight.

A small chirping sounded in Kirk's ear and he acknowledged the signal from the sniper team that they were in position.

A soft breeze blew through the night and Kirk used the sound for cover as he shifted his weight and stood in the shadows to the left of the window. He saw the shadows of four men moving in the alleyway. He recognized Monte and his usual guards. "This is One. Monte is in place."

"Confirm when target enters."

"I will. One out."

Olivia didn't know what to expect when Kirk and the others went into the neighborhood they had. She sat quietly in the passenger seat of the Humvee. Laz had his window down and stared out at the night. He was listening intently to the chatter on the radio. She was incredibly nervous about Kirk because he wasn't with her.

A gunshot shattered the night sounds and Laz slumped forward over the wheel of the car. Olivia started to scream, but then realized that wasn't going to help.

"Get out of the car," Laz said. His voice was low and raspy. "Stay down so no one can see you."

She nodded and opened her door, dropping to the ground and crawling away from the vehicle into the shadows.

Olivia heard the sound of men's voices approaching the Humvee. "I saw Olivia in here. Where is she?"

It was Ray. Dammmit, had she compromised the mission coming along with them?

"She's not in the vehicle," Burati said.

She guessed that Burati had gotten out of jail thanks to Ray. Her mind raced with scenarios and backup plans, but she had

no idea how to make them happen. There was no backup plan
that would work.

"Is he still alive?" Ray asked.

"Yes, Mr. Ray," Burati said.

"Where did she go?" Ray asked Laz.

Laz gave him the finger and Ray backhanded him. "Kill
him. Then help me find her. She can't have gone far."

She was on her own and determined not to need rescuing
this time. She'd picked up a few things from the fights she'd
been in. She took a deep breath and knew that this was the
kind of situation that she really excelled at. She'd wait until
she had an opening and make her move. She'd beaten Lambert once before, she'd damn well do it again.

She heard the sound of a gunshot and almost cried when
she realized that Laz was probably dead.

"No more screw-ups like the last time," Lambert said.

"I didn't screw that up," Burati said.

She eased her way away from the vehicle toward the alleyway.

"I don't want excuses," Lambert said.

"I thought this mess with Monte was your key to a new life
outside of the Diamond mine."

Lambert turned on Burati, grabbing the other man by the
neck and squeezing. Burati tried to shrink back from him, but
could only flail around trying to breathe. "Don't think. I'm not
paying you to do that. Just follow orders."

Lambert pushed Burati away. "Yes, sir," Burati said. A bead
of sweat formed on his temple and rolled down the side of his
face.

"Just find that bitch Olivia."

"I found her," Burati said looking straight at her.

Olivia ran flat out as fast as she could. She stayed in the
shadows that stretched into long dark spots at the end of the

alley and eased herself around the corner. She held her breath to listen for the sounds of the men following her.

She heard Ray and Burati come down the alley. She stayed where she was, trying desperately to be quiet.

She heard someone moving toward her from the other direction and almost screamed when a hand fell heavy on her shoulder. But another hand covered her mouth and she twisted her head to see Kirk there next to her.

Olivia wrapped her arms around Kirk, hugging him to her for just a quick minute. She almost lost her composure seeing him here when the odds were so stacked against her.

He wore desert camouflage and some paint on his face. He looked like the cold-blooded killer that she knew he could be. For the first time she saw him as a mercenary and she thanked God he was one. She knew this was just another glimpse of the man she loved.

But then she pushed away from him, staring up into his eyes, needing to pass as much information to him as she could before Burati and Ray found them.

Kirk rubbed his finger down the side of her face. She flinched as he encountered a bruise she hadn't realized she had.

He pulled her to him and gently kissed the bruised area of her face. She felt so cherished and safe with him here. Like now she could do anything. She wasn't afraid now. With Kirk by her side, she knew they would get the bad guys.

"Are all the guys with you?" she asked, trying to keep her voice low. She liked to know the odds. She didn't want to get in his way. "He killed Laz."

"You don't need to fight. I can take Ray out from here," Kirk said. "You have more bumps and bruises than I like to see on you."

"That's good, because I'm one big ache." She swallowed hard. "But I don't want you to shoot Ray. I know that's your job and you are good at it, but I want Ray to go to jail for killing that man."

Kirk pulled her back into his arms. "I will do my best not to kill him."

"I'm fine." She wasn't sure if she was telling the truth or just lying to make him feel better.

"I'm here now, so you don't have to worry about anything else."

She glanced into his eyes and saw the truth there. They were partners in this and he wasn't going to lie even to make her feel better.

"Tell me what you need me to do."

"Do you have any weapons on you?"

"No." She felt so silly that she hadn't been prepared. Kirk removed his knife sheath, handing it to Olivia. She tucked it into the back of her pants.

"Do you want a handgun?" he asked, holding out a small semiautomatic.

She shook her head. She couldn't handle a weapon and she certainly wasn't a marksman. Even the knife had her a little worried.

Kirk rubbed her arm in a strong massaging motion that hurt at first but then lessened the pain in her arm. "Thanks, that feels so much better now."

He kissed her. "When this is over, I'll take all your pain away."

Kirk drew his Sig-Sauer and eased out of the shadows. Though his training was as a sniper, he was just as lethal up close, and he wasn't going to be separated from Olivia again. He'd almost had a heart attack when Savage had let them know that she was in trouble. This was the hardest part. He heard the whoosh and swish of a bullet behind fired from a silencer. The bullet missed Lambert and alerted the man to their presence.

"Find her, Burati," Lambert said. "I think she is over there."

Kirk knew the other man was really working for Phillip and would have protected Olivia. He probably should have mentioned that to her. "Burati works for your cousin. He won't harm you."

"What? I want to know about this," she said. "He killed Laz."

"Laz isn't dead. We can talk this through later."

Kirk waited for the chirping signal of his men and as soon as he heard it, he stepped out of the bushes with his weapon drawn.

Lambert glanced at Kirk in full desert camouflage and face paint.

Burati stood between Kirk and Lambert, using his body as a shield.

"Fuck. I want Olivia. I'll kill you if I have to," Lambert said.

"You aren't getting her," Kirk said.

"Kill him," Ray said to Burati. But Burati turned and lifted his weapon toward Ray.

Lambert didn't hesitate a second when he realized his man wasn't going to follow orders. Kirk held his breath as Ray lifted his own gun and shot Burati, hitting Burati in the center of his chest.

"Oh, God, you killed him," Olivia screamed jumping out of the shadows.

Lambert was distracted by Olivia's screams. Kirk moved quickly to Lambert's right side and turned sideways. Leading with his left foot, he stepped diagonally toward Lambert, keeping his shooting arm directly in front of him. He grabbed

Lambert's wrist with his left hand, bringing his weapon up toward Lambert's face.

Lambert brought his left hand up in a crosscut punch that knocked Kirk's head back. He held tight to Lambert's wrist, pivoting on his left foot and breaking Kirk's grip on his arm.

"Don't move or you're next," Lambert said, raising his weapon. Kirk was in point-blank range. He took two steps backwards, bringing his handgun up.

"This looks like a stalemate to me," Lambert said.

"Don't bet on it," Kirk said.

"Who the hell are you?"

"The Savage Seven," Kirk said. "We've got you surrounded. There's no one coming to help. Drop your weapon and surrender."

"Surrender isn't an option," Lambert said.

"Fine by me," Kirk said, lifting his gun and firing at Ray.

Ray fired not at Kirk but at Olivia. In that moment Kirk's entire life flashed before his eyes. And no matter what Olivia had asked him, he wasn't going to let this man live. He took a deep breath and narrowed his eyes. He let half of the breath out and pulled the trigger.

Ray crumpled to the ground dead.

Olivia screamed but stayed where she was with Burati. Savage and the other men moved in. Kirk's entire body ached from head to toe, but when Olivia sank down next to him, her small arms wrapping around his waist, he felt a wave of peace wash over him.

It took three days of wrangling, but Kirk was finally free to leave Jo'burg. Olivia had stayed at the jail where he was held until the authorities had conducted their investigation of the death of Ray Lambert. The information that Burati, Phillip, and Kirk had gathered all came into play and eventually he was released.

Laz was in the hospital recovering from his wounds, as was Burati. But both men would live—something that meant the world to Olivia. Her parents had flown in to see her and if all went well she and Kirk would be joining them for dinner tonight.

She felt safe knowing that Ray couldn't hurt her again, but a part of her knew she'd never go back to being the woman she was before.

"What are you doing here?" Kirk asked as he walked out of the station house.

"Waiting for you," she said.

"Why?"

"Because . . . I love you, Kirk, and I don't want to let you go."

"That wasn't love—it was lust."

"Maybe at first, but it's been three days since I've seen you and I . . . I've missed you."

He shrugged.

"Don't do that. I think I mean more to you than just some hot lay you had during a job."

He wasn't going to say anything, she thought. She saw it in his eyes.

"Dammit, Kirk. I thought Ray took everything from me and you are the man who made me realize that safety wasn't something that could come from a place or from money. Safety for me comes from being with you."

"Ah, baby. You'll get over that."

"No. I won't. I know what I need and that is you, Kirk Mann."

He shook his head. "No, you don't."

He walked away, and Olivia knew she had no choice but to let him go.

Chapter Twenty-three

Kirk watched Olivia as she moved through the crowded room. He'd gotten her message through Anna that she needed him. That someone was threatening her safety. But there wasn't anyone here who would harm her. It was a party in her honor.

A launch party for her latest book.

She glanced up and saw him and smiled.

She came over to his side and wrapped her arms around him. God, she felt good. The last two missions they'd been on had been hard and long. And he'd done his job. He was too good at it not to, but he'd missed her.

"I missed you," she said.

"I thought you were in danger."

"I am. Danger of losing my heart. I know you thought my feelings would go away, but they haven't and they won't."

"Do you really believe that?"

"Yes. I do."

"Then let's get out of here," he said.

He took her back to his flat. "I missed you."

"Of course you did. We're meant to be together."

"I can't stop doing my job," he said.

"I won't ask you to. I just need you in my life. I love you, Kirk, and without you I'm not ever going to feel alive."

"I love you, too, Olivia. I don't know how it happened, but I think it might have started when you sang in the car."

"No, it wasn't then. You were annoyed with me then."

"I'm not annoyed now," he said, kissing her. He carried her down the hall.

He couldn't fight her and his own instincts, which had told him leaving her in South Africa had been a mistake. He bent down and took her mouth with his, letting his hands wander over her body.

He pulled her closer to him. Felt her fingers tracing over his chest, her fingers lingering on the puckered flesh over his breastbone. They undressed each other slowly.

"This is new. What's this from?" she asked.

"Gunshot." He'd taken that bullet back in a raid on a rebel camp on their last mission.

She leaned down and laved at the new scar tissue with her tongue. Then kissed him lightly. "I'm sorry you were hurt."

She wrapped her arms around him, and he slowly turned so she could touch his back. She found each of his scars and caressed them. Held the pain that had lingered in his soul with her innocent touch.

He caressed the long length of her back and the edge of her panties. He slipped his finger under the elastic band and felt the cool skin at the small of her back.

She shivered with awareness and nestled closer to him, tilting her head back and looking up at him. There were questions in her eyes and he knew this was going to complicate things endlessly, but he needed her. And for the first time in a long time he was going to take what he wanted. Not because he was being paid to do it but because he needed it.

He kissed her again and let the passion he'd felt for her flow through him. He brought one hand around her waist, ran it up her body, and cupped her breasts.

They were full without being too large and her nipples were a pretty pink color that matched her lips. He leaned down and dropped a kiss on each one. They both puckered up and she let her breath out on a sigh.

He rubbed his finger over her left nipple while he took her mouth with his again. She tasted right, he thought. Like no other woman had before. Normally he wasn't a big kisser, but with Olivia, he needed to feel her mouth under his. Needed to taste her. And let her taste him.

He took his time with her nipples, arousing her slowly with his hands before moving down and suckling on each of them. He moved down her body, caressing the small curve of her stomach and using his teeth to scrape gently around her belly button. She shifted on the bed, her hips lifting. He smoothed his hand down toward the apex of her thighs, taking his time to caress her thighs and then the lower curve of her belly. Running his hand all over her body but avoiding her center.

"Touch me, Kirk," she said.

He shook his head, dropping a quick nibbling kiss on her mouth before shifting so that he was crouched between her legs. He took the edge of her panties in his hands and drew them down her legs. He tossed them on the floor, leaving her bare in front of him. He shifted her on the bed so she was more in the center of it. He was fully aroused, and she hesitated as she glanced down at his erection. Then he felt her fingers on him, her touch as she caressed him, undid him.

Her legs moved restlessly on the bed, drawing his attention back to her feminine mound. He needed to touch her.

He lay next to her again and stroked his hands down her curvy body. He reached her mound and slowly parted her lower lips, revealing her very pink flesh. He touched her lightly and she moaned.

"Did that hurt?"

"No," she said, shaking her head.

He leaned down and kissed her, stroking her mouth lightly with his tongue. She tasted good as he continued to stroke her body.

She lifted her hips toward his touch. He slipped his fingers lower, finding the moisture at her center, rubbing her soft skin as he pushed her legs farther apart until he could reach her dewy core. He pushed his finger into her body and drew out some of her slickness; he lifted his head and looked up her body.

Her eyes were closed. Her head tipped back, her shoulders arched, throwing her breasts forward with their berry-hard tips, begging for more attention. Her entire body was a creamy delight.

He lowered his head again, hungry for more of her. He feasted on her mouth the way a starving man would. He used his fingers to bring her to the brink of climax but held her there, wanting to draw out the moment of completion until she was begging him for it.

Her hands left her body and grasped his head as she thrust her hips up toward his face. But he pulled back so that she didn't get the contact she craved.

"Kirk, please."

He scraped his nail over her clitoris and she screamed as her orgasm rocked through her body. He kept his mouth on hers until her body stopped shuddering, holding the kiss while her body still pulsed.

"I love you, Olivia."

"I know."

He smacked her on the butt. "Do you know I'm going to marry you?"

"Yes, I do."

Don't miss Shannon McKenna's latest,
TASTING FEAR, out now from Brava . . .

Liam sounded exhausted. Fed up. She didn't blame him a bit. She was a piece of work. Her mind raced, to come up with a plausible lie. Letting him see how small she felt would just embarrass them both.

She shook her head. "Nothing," she whispered.

He let out a sigh, and leaned back, leaning his head against the back of the couch. Covering his eyes with his hands.

That was when she noticed the condition of his hand. His knuckles were torn and raw, encrusted with blood. God, she hadn't even given a thought for his injuries, his trauma, his shock. She'd just zoned out, floated in her bubble, leaned on him. As if he were an oak.

But he wasn't an oak. He was a man. He'd fought like a demon for her, and risked his life, and gotten hurt, and she was so freaked out and self-absorbed, she hadn't even noticed. She was mortified.

"Liam. Your hand," she fussed, getting up. "Let me get some disinfectant, and some—"

"It's OK," he muttered. "Forget about it."

"Like hell! You're bleeding!" She bustled around, muttering and scolding to hide her own discomfiture, gathering gauze and cotton balls and antibiotic ointment. He let her fuss, a martyred look on his face. After she'd finished taping his hand, she looked at his battered face and grabbed a handful of his polo. "What about the rest of you?"

"Just some bruises," he hedged.

"Where?" she persisted, tugging at his shirt. "Show me."

He wrenched the fabric out of her hand. "If I take off my clothes now, it's not going to be to show you my bruises," he said.

She blinked, swallowed, tried to breathe. Reorganized her mind. There it was. Finally verbalized. No more glossing over it, running away.

"After all this?" Her tone was timid. "You still want to . . . now?"

"Fuck, yes." His tone was savage. "I've wanted it since I laid eyes on you. It's gotten worse ever since. And combat adrenaline gives a guy a hard-on like a railroad spike, even if there weren't a beautiful woman in my face, driving me fucking nuts. Which puts me in a bad place, Nancy. I know the timing sucks for you. The timing's been piss poor since we met, but it never gets any better. It just keeps getting worse."

"Hey. It's OK." She patted his back with a shy, nervous hand. He was usually so calm, so controlled. It unnerved her to see him agitated.

He didn't seem to hear her. "And the worse it gets, the worse I want it," he went on, his voice harsh. "Which makes me feel like a jerk, and a user, and an asshole. Promising to protect you—"

"You did protect me," she reminded him.

"Yeah, and I told you it wasn't an exchange. You don't owe me sex. You don't owe me anything. And that really fucks me up. Because I can't even remove myself from the situation. I'm scared to death to leave you alone. And that puts me between a rock and a hard place."

She put her finger over his mouth. "Wow," she murmured. "I had no idea you could get worked into such a state. Mr. Super-mellow Liam let's-contemplate-the-beauty-of-the-flower Knightly."

His explosive snort of derision cut her off. She shushed him again, enjoying the feel of his lips beneath her finger. "You're not a jerk or a user," she said gently. "You were magnificent. Thank you. Again."

He looked away. There was a brief, embarrassed pause. "That's very generous of you," he said, trying to flex the wounded hand. "But I'm not fishing for compliments."

"I never thought that you were." She placed her own hand below his, and rested them both gently on his thigh. Her fingers dug into the thick muscle of his quadriceps, through the dirty, bloodstained denim of his jeans. Beneath the fabric, he was so hot. So strong and solid.

She moved her hand up, slowly but surely, stroking higher towards his groin. His breath caught, and then stopped entirely as her fingers brushed the turgid bulge of his penis beneath the fabric.

Here went nothing. "I think I know what you mean, about the hard place," she whispered, swirling her fingertips over it. Wow. A lot of him. That thick, broad, hard stalk just went on and on. "Or was this what you meant when you were referring to the rock?"

His face was a mask of tension, neck muscles clenched, tendons standing out. "You don't have to do this," he said, his voice strangled.

Aw. So sweet. Her fingers closed around him, squeezing. He groaned, and a shudder jarred his body. "I can't seem to stop," she said.

"Watch out, Nancy," he said hoarsely. "If you start something now, there's no stopping it."

She stroked him again, deeper, tighter, a slow caress that

wrung a keening gasp from his throat. "I know," she said. "I know."

He reached out, a little awkwardly, clasping his arms around her shoulders, staring into her eyes as if expecting her to bolt.

He pulled her close, enfolding her in his warmth, his power.

Suddenly, they were kissing. She had no idea who had kissed who. The kiss was desperate, achingly sweet. Not a power struggle, not a matter of talent or skill, just a hunger to get as close as two humans could be. He held her like he was afraid she'd be torn away from him.

Upcoming courses include
PRIDE AND PASSION by Sylvia Day.
Turn the page for a preview!

"What type of individual would you consider ideal to play this role of suitor/protector/investigator?" Jasper asked finally.

Eliza's head tilted slightly as she pondered her answer. "He should be quiet, even-tempted, and a proficient dancer."

"How do dullness and the ability to dance signify in catching a possible murderer?" he queried, scowling.

"I did not say 'dull,' Mr. Bond. Kindly do not put words into my mouth. In order to be seen as a true threat for my attentions, he should be someone that everyone would believe I would be attracted to."

"You are not attracted to handsome men?"

"Mr. Bond, I dislike being rude. However, you leave me no choice. The point of fact is that you clearly are not marriage material."

"I am quite relieved to hear a female recognize that," he drawled.

"How could anyone doubt it?" She made a sweeping gesture with her hand. "I can more easily picture you in a sword-fight or fisticuffs than I can see you enjoying an afternoon of croquet or after dinner chess. I am an intellectual, sir. And while I do not mean to say that you are lacking in mental acuity, you are obviously built for more physically strenuous pursuits."

"I see."

"Why, anyone would take one look at you and ascertain that you are not like the others at all! It would be evident straightaway that I would never consider a man such as you with even remote seriousness. Quite frankly, sir, you are not my type of male."

A slow smile began in his dark eyes, then moved downward to curve his lips. It was arresting. Slightly wicked. Troublesome.

Eliza did not like trouble overmuch.

He glanced at her uncle, the earl. "Please forgive me, my lord, but I must speak bluntly in regards to this subject. Most especially because this is a matter of life and death."

"Quite right," Melville agreed. "Straight to the point, I always say. Time is too precious to waste on inanities."

"Agreed." Jasper glanced back at Eliza, his mischievous smile widening. "Miss Martin, forgive me, but I must point out that your inexperience is limiting your understanding of the situation."

"Inexperience with what?"

"Men. More precisely, gold digging men."

"I would have you know," she retorted, bristling, "that in my six years on the marriage market I have had more than enough experience with gentlemen in want of funds."

"Then why," he drawled, "do you not know that they are successful for reasons far removed from social suitability?"

Eliza blinked. "I beg your pardon?"

"Women do not marry gold diggers because they can dance and sit quietly. They marry them for their appearance and physical prowess—two attributes you have already established that I have."

"I do not see—"

"Clearly, you do not, so I shall explain." His smile continued to grow. "Gold diggers who flourish do not strive to satisfy a woman's intellectual needs. Those can be met through friends and acquaintances. They do not seek to provide the type of companionship one enjoys in social settings or with a game table between them. Again, there are others who can do so."

"Mr. Bond—"

"No, they strive to satisfying the only position that is theirs alone, a position that some men make no effort to excel in. So rare is the skill, that many a woman will disregard other considerations in favor of it."

She growled softly. "Will you get to the point, please?"

"Fornication," his lordship said, before returning to mumbling to himself.

Eliza shot to her feet. "I beg your pardon?"

As courtesy dictated, both her uncle and Jasper rose along with her.

"I prefer to call it 'seduction,'" Jasper said, his eyes laughing.

"I call it ridiculous," she rejoined, hands on her hips. "In the grand scheme of life, do you collect how little time a person spends abed when compared to other activities?"

His gaze dropped to her hips. The smile became a full-blown grin. "That truly depends on who else is occupying said bed."

"Dear heavens." Eliza shivered at the look Jasper was giving her now. It was certainly *not* a bug-under-the-glass look. No, it was more triumphant. Challenged. Anticipatory. For some unknown, godforsaken reason she had managed to prod the man's damnable masculine pride into action. "While I acknowledge that a man's brain might reverse such channels of thought, I cannot see a woman's doing so."

"But is it not men whom you wish to affect with this scheme?"

She bit her lower lip. Clever, clever man. He knew quite well that she had no idea how men's minds worked. She had no notion of whether he was correct, or simply tenacious about securing work.

"Give me a sennight," he offered. "One week to prove both my point and competency. If at the end you do not agree with one or the other, I will accept no payment for services rendered."

And here's a preview from
SEDUCING THE MOON by Sherrill Quinn,
out now from Brava . . .

Declan O'Connell paused next to a large tree. Bending slightly, he braced himself with one palm on the rough bark and tried to catch his breath. He'd been at a full-out run for half an hour, testing the limits of his new metabolism.

His new *werewolf* metabolism.

In seconds his breathing was back to normal. He straightened. At times it hardly seemed possible that it had been four months since he'd been bitten, since his life had been turned upside down. Other times it seemed like he'd been this way all his life.

He didn't know why his friend Ryder kicked up such a fuss about it. Ryder Merrick had been a werewolf for nearly twenty years now. He'd been adamant that Declan learn how to control the beast within, stressing that the urge to shift could come upon him quite unexpectedly, especially at times of high emotion.

Declan frowned. He hadn't been so sure about that when Ryder had first said it, and he wasn't so sure about it now. He'd always been able to keep a cap on his emotions, especially during crises. Even with only having lived with this . . . condition for four months, he'd been able to control when he shifted. But he hadn't been able to stop the shift partway, becoming something not quite wolf but not fully man, either.

Ryder, as someone who had become a werewolf due to his bloodlines, was incapable of becoming a wolf-man. When he shifted, he went from human to wolf almost faster than the eye could follow.

Declan, being a werewolf through the bite of another, would eventually be able to turn into a wolf-man, though he hadn't yet mastered the ability.

Concentrating, he stared at his right hand and tried to make just his hand morph into that of a wolf-man. His fingertips tingled, sharp pain throbbed in the joints as if with the onset of arthritis, but nothing else happened.

At least, nothing worth much—his nails darkened and, perhaps, looked a little longer, but his hands were still human-looking.

So, no luck with a partial shift.

Yet.

He knew with enough determination he would eventually figure it out. It would just take more practice.

He *was* certain he had achieved the restraint needed to control the shift to his wolf form. Except for the three nights of the full moon. During those nights it was impossible to resist the metamorphosis into wolf, and equally impossible to shift back to human until the morning sun forced the moon to give up its hold in the heavens.

He glanced up at the robin's egg blue sky. Toward the east he could see the half moon, clearly visible in daylight. Just one more week until the full moon . . .

He could hear the lap of the ocean against the shore and jogged down the path, leaving the wooded area and venturing onto the rocky shore. He focused his attention westward and, with the enhanced vision of his inner wolf, could make out the larger island of St. Mary's in the distance.

St. Mary's, the biggest island in the Isles of Scilly off the coast of Cornwall. St. Mary's, where Pelicia was.

Where his heart was.

It was time to go get it back and claim his mate.

Pelicia wouldn't know what hit her.